poison

Alex,
Hope you
enjoy
ElReed

Books by EL Reed

Hatchet

Spikes

Books by Emma Leigh Reed

Making the Rules

Breaking the Rules

A Fine Line

A Time to Heal

Second Chances

Trusting Love

Mirrrored Deception

poison

E.L. REED

ELRpublishing

Text copyright © 2023 by E.L. Reed

Published by ELR Publishing.

ISBN-13: 978-1-944550-19-6

Cover and interior design by Kenny Holcomb

Printed in the United States of America

To Aubrey

May your fearlessness bring you
many adventures

one

I sat at the table as I crushed the arsenic crystals with my mortar and pestle. My latex-glove-covered hands moved in rhythm as I wondered how I even knew that arsenic was the poison to use for killing the men who had rejected me. Once the crystals were crushed, I placed the powder into several small, glass pill bottles, measuring each dose to three grams.

I leaned back and closed my eyes. Frustration had grown with seeing that bitch get what she wanted. No one even cared who she hurt in the meantime. She thought of only herself, and I was sick of it. It was time someone taught her a lesson. If life had taught me anything, it was that I couldn't sit back and expect a man to materialize on my doorstep. If you wanted the perfect man—the romantic life you thought you deserved—you had to flirt that man right into your life. Beautiful women had a habit of taking those men away without even trying.

I don't know how I instinctively knew that this drug would have excellent results... *where did that come from...* and could be the one that kept me from getting caught.

My thoughts continued to hatch a plan of revenge. There were many, men and women, who had done enough to hurt me, and I wouldn't stand for it anymore. I intended to fight back and put them where they belonged. And if I could damage *her* in the meantime, that would be the icing on the cake.

I reached for the wooden box on the table and flipped open the cover. Multiple gold wedding rings lay inside. They were for the perfect men in my life. One by one, I would find a man and make him mine... until death do us part... how short that may ever be. I smiled as I fingered the rings and allowed my mind to drift to all the romantic stories I read and how much I wanted that in my life. My father had kept me from living a life full of romance, never allowing me to wear makeup or dress attractively. His warped sense of "men won't molest women who aren't attractive" had driven me nuts, and the longing for love and romance in my life just increased despite his best-laid efforts to shield me from men.

I stood and slipped into my pocket a small vial of the powder. It was time to pick up my honey's coffee, as was my habit. Lately, he had been pulling away. He had told me he and his wife were not getting along. I also knew that he saw that bitch for events; I was furious that he would not take me! Apparently, I was good enough for sex, but nothing else. He went on and on about the intelligent conversations he had with *her*.

By the time I reached the coffee stand, I was fuming with the unfairness of my life and my efforts going unnoticed with Sam. I ordered two coffees and moved to the side to add cream and sugar. In Sam's coffee, I added two creams and one sugar, as well as the powder from the vial in my pocket. I stirred them and was pleased to see how well it dissolved in the hot liquid, then strolled toward his office, slyly smiling.

"Mr. Porter is unavailable," his secretary greeted me as I strolled into the office.

"That's okay," I answered. "I'll just leave this for him." I set the coffee on her desk. She nodded and smiled, assuring me he would get it.

I left the office and turned toward home. I needed to change and get ready to meet a friend for drinks. My heart raced with anticipation of when I would hear that Sam Porter was dead. I had planned it out to the minute on my end, but it all hinged on him drinking his coffee. He was a creature of habit and always had coffee before he met with her. It would be hard to explain a death in her presence.

Sara opened the door and saw Sam standing outside, leaning heavily against the doorframe. She immediately reached for him. "What's wrong?" He looked pale, and she feared he couldn't stand on his own.

"Not feeling well. On the way over here, my stomach got really queasy."

Sara helped him to the couch and placed a pillow behind his head. She grabbed a trash can and placed it next to him. "Let me get you some water."

With a glass of water in one hand and a bottle of ibuprofen and one of antacids in the other; she returned to the living room. Sam was lying on his side on the couch in a fetal position, holding onto his stomach. Before she could hand him the glass of water, he started vomiting. Sara dropped the glass and bottles, reached for the trash can, and held it while

E.L. Reed

Sam hurled the contents of his stomach. By the time he finished, sweat poured off him.

"I should head home." Sam attempted to stand, but he suddenly clutched his chest. He quickly went down to the floor. Sara dropped beside him and grabbed his shoulders.

"Sam... Sam..." She shook him.

No response.

Sara jumped up, ran to the table to grab her cell-phone, and punched in 9-1-1.

"Nine-one-one. What's your emergency?"

"I need an ambulance at 412 Garden Terrace in Deep River. There's a man here I think is having a heart attack."

"What's your name?"

"Sara Wesley."

"Is this your residence, ma'am?"

"Yes, please hurry."

"What can you tell me about the man that needs medical assistance?"

"His name is Sam Porter. He's forty-five years old."

"Hold on while I dispatch an ambulance." Sara sat there holding Sam's hand while she waited for the operator to come back on. "Sara, are you with me?"

"Yes."

"Okay, the ambulance is four minutes out."

Everything became a blur from the moment the ambulance arrived and Sara let in the paramedics. She stood to the side of the room while they worked on Sam. By the time they'd arrived, he was barely breathing. They loaded him into the ambulance.

"Can I follow?" Sara asked. She didn't know what she was supposed to do and felt she should call Sam's wife, but that would be an awkward conversation.

"Yes, ma'am," the attendant called over his shoulder as he closed the ambulance door.

☠   ☠   ☠

Sara was pacing in the waiting room of the hospital when Sam's wife walked in. Two police officers followed directly behind her. Apparently, the police had gone and told her what had happened. Sara slid into a chair. She hoped *the wife* did not see her while she walked to the receptionist and asked to speak to the doctor treating her husband.

Sara slowly stood and inched her way toward the door.

"Wait!" the wife called out just as Sara had almost exited the room.

She froze. The policeman moved to the doorway as Mrs. Porter approached Sara.

"Were you with him?" she demanded.

Sara nodded. "He had just arrived at my place, and he said he wasn't feeling well, even before he got there."

"Right." The woman sneered at Sara, then politely acknowledged the police officer, who stepped up next to Sara.

"Miss, can we speak outside, please?" The officer's voice was soft, but firm.

"Of course," Sara managed to say and turned to walk in front of him. She glanced back, but Sam's wife was already headed for a chair to sit in. Sara walked outside and faced the police officer.

"Ma'am, Mr. Porter has passed, and I would like you to come with me to the police station for questioning."

"I didn't do anything to him."

"Please ma'am." The police officer gestured to the door.

Sara shrugged. "I have nothing to hide. Can I drive my car and follow you?"

"Yes."

Sara turned without a word and strode to her car.

This was ridiculous. What more could she possibly tell them? The way that the police had followed Sam's wife into the hospital, surely the woman must have accused her of something. Sara paused with her hand on the door handle. *Sam passed. Sam's dead.* The realization hit hard, and she leaned against the car, tears filling her eyes. Sam was gone, just like that.

The police car drove up beside her. "You all right?" the officer called through his open passenger window.

"Yes." Sara opened the door. "I'll follow you," she said and slipped into the car.

two

Dawson grabbed the folder off his desk and headed to interrogation room one. The person he was about to question had been with the victim. He peeked at the folder and saw the name, Sara Wesley. He opened the door and stepped in. The woman stood with her back to him, looking out the window. She turned slowly and Dawson stopped in his tracks.

"Sara?" The word felt like sandpaper on his throat.

She tentatively smiled. "Hi, Wes."

He threw the folder on the table and stared at her. With a shake of his head, he tried to reign in control. "*Hi, Wes.* After all these years, that is what you have to say to me?"

"I told you I was fine. You just kept being pigheaded and roaming the streets. No one asked you to do that."

Dawson scoffed. "Yes, wouldn't want anyone to *actually* show they care about you. I guess when you walked out on everyone, you walked out for good." He ran his fingers through his hair, trying to find something to do with his hands when all he wanted to do was throttle her.

"It wasn't like that, Wes, and you know it." Her voice was soft.

"Have a seat, Ms. *Wesley*, is it? Not Dawson?" He slid into a chair, ignoring her last comment.

"I choose to go by Wesley instead of Dawson. It's a name that has special meaning to me." She took the chair across from him.

Dawson ignored her. "So, you were with the victim. What's your connection to him?"

"We see each other occasionally. He hires me to attend functions with him when his wife is unavailable."

Dawson looked up at her. "You work as a prostitute?"

"Are you kidding me?" Her voice rose an octave. "I am *not* a prostitute. You, of all people, should know me better than that."

"I don't know you at all." He flipped a sheet in the folder. "How long have you been selling yourself for money?"

He raised his eyes to meet hers. He knew he sounded cold and like a jerk, but he was mad. He would be damned if she thought she could be a suspect for a murder and believe he'd just walk in there, forgive everything, and be on her side. He had a job to do and did not want to be bothered by dealing with hookers.

Sara stood up fast, and the chair fell back to the floor with a thud. "I don't sell my body for money. I work as an escort. The men I am with, I provide a service to keep them company. We go out to dinner—I attend functions with them. There is not an agreement for sex." She turned back toward the window, muttering "you prick," under her breath.

Dawson easily heard her and couldn't help but allow a small smile to flicker. He had gotten under her skin. She was still the hot-tempered sister he used to needle when they were younger. "I'm just doing my job," he said as his smile faded, "and yes, sometimes being a prick is part of it."

She spun around, wide-eyed. "I didn't call you a—"

"Yes, you did." He stood and grabbed the folder. "Just sit tight."

He left the room before she could say another word and strode to his desk. He reached for his phone to call Ali, but before he could even start, she walked in.

"Hey. I heard there was a suspect already."

Dawson shook his head. "You have impeccable timing. You will never guess who the suspect is."

She quizzically tilted her head at him. "Do I *need* to guess?"

"Sara." The word hung between them as Ali stared at him and Dawson watched her.

"Oh, I don't suppose your first meeting between the two of you went well." She smiled. "I can only imagine your reaction to seeing her. Did you lose it on her for not actually talking to you instead of just leaving notes?"

Dawson rolled his eyes. "Why would you assume I would lose it?" He placed his right hand over his heart. "I am always the kind soul that puts others first."

Ali burst into laughter. "Yeah, okay. I'm sorry. Who are you and where is my darling boyfriend?"

"Whatever." Dawson pulled her close for a quick hug. "Want to come back in and talk to her with me? Have you started the autopsy yet?"

"Yes, and no." Sara smiled. "Yes, I want to meet her and listen in on the interrogation, and no, I haven't started the autopsy yet. Tomorrow morning."

Dawson tilted his head. "Come on then."

They proceeded back to the interrogation room and when they entered, they found Sara sitting at the table, waiting.

Sara stood. "You must be Ali."

Ali nodded. "Hi, Sara."

"This isn't a social visit," Dawson broke in.

Sara turned toward him. "Of course not." She slid back into the chair. "Can we at least be civil while we do this?"

Dawson sat down. "Not sure civil is part of my job."

Ali glared at him. "Well, since you are a public servant, I would say it is exactly part of your job."

Dawson grimaced. "Fine." He turned his attention to Sara. "Please state your full *legal* name, and how you became known as the name you use now, as well as any other aliases you have."

"Sara Dawson. I started using Sara Wesley shortly after I left home, mostly because I hoped it would throw my family off from finding me. I opened my escort business shortly after my boyfriend and I broke up."

"And when was that?" Dawson didn't look at her but was busy taking notes.

"About six months after I left home."

He glanced up at those words. "And how long have you known the victim?"

"About three years. I started working with him to go to functions that his wife couldn't attend with him, like I said. We enjoyed each other's company, and it just continued from there. We would go out to dinner, occasionally a movie, but a lot of times, we just hung out and talked."

"And what are your rates for these services?"

Dawson could feel Ali's eyes on him. He knew she didn't approve of his questions, and they weren't totally necessary, but Dawson needed more information about her life the past few years.

"Is that really important to the case?" Sara asked.

Dawson just looked up and stared at her—face completely neutral—and waited.

"I have an hourly rate and it depends on the client. He was a long-time client, so he paid two hundred and fifty dollars an hour. My newer clients pay upwards of five hundred dollars an hour."

"Sounds like prostitution to me," Dawson muttered.

Ali touched his arm and Dawson sat back. He knew what Ali was doing, and she was right, of course. He was being a jerk because he was angry with his sister. Ali always had that effect on him... she knew what he needed when he needed it, and how to force him to take a break and think without telling him to do it.

"He didn't feel well when he got to my place," Sara said in almost a whisper. "When I opened the door, he was leaning against the frame, holding his stomach. He had been there long when he said he wasn't feeling that great and was tingly all over. He laid down on the couch. I put a cold compress on his head, hoping to help. Almost immediately he said he didn't feel well, he started vomiting. He got up to head to the bathroom, grabbed his chest and fainted. That's when I called 9-1-1. It took them about ten minutes to get there. He never regained consciousness and apparently died before they got him to the hospital." Her voice cracked as she finished speaking, tears filling her eyes.

"Apparently?" Ali asked.

"I found out at the hospital from the police officer who asked me to come here that he had passed. No one at the hospital would tell me anything."

Dawson pushed the box of tissues on the table toward her.

"Thank you." She pulled one from the box and blotted her eyes.

"Where were you before he showed up?" Dawson asked.

"I was with my friend, Evie. Evelyn Lancaster. We had gone out for a drink at the Fuzzy Navel. We walked back to my place where she had left her car about ten minutes before he arrived. Evie left me at the front door as she continued on to her car in the parking lot, and I went upstairs. Sam and I had nothing to eat or drink. He immediately said he didn't feel good and just wanted to lie down before he went home. We were going to cancel the evening."

"I will need Evie's number and address so I can contact her to corroborate your story."

"Okay."

Dawson looked at Ali and raised an eyebrow in question. She shook her head.

"You are free to go, but make sure you stick around town and be available if we have more questions."

"I will." Sara stood. "Wes, I'm sorry."

He appraised her and gave a small nod before opening the door to let her pass through.

Dawson glanced over at Ali, still sitting at the table. "What do you think?" He walked back to the table and sat down, facing her.

"I think you were a little tough on her," Ali said.

"Not what I meant. Did she do it?"

"Wes..." Ali's voice was soft, and her hand reached for his. "You can't ignore this. She's your sister."

He closed his eyes and sighed. "I know. I'm just so mad at her for the way she acts, so blasé about this." He looked at Ali. "Was I truly not supposed to search for my sister?"

Ali just stared at him in a way he knew well. There was no right answer to this. Sara probably would have been upset if he hadn't looked. By the notes she had left for him, it seemed Sara wanted a connection with him as much as he had wanted it, but neither of them knew how to go about reconnecting.

three

Ali walked into the morgue early. It had been a long night. She and Wes had talked long into the night about how best to proceed with Sara. Wes wanted to walk away and ignore her, "two can play that game," he had said. Ali smirked. Sometimes he was so stubborn, she just didn't know what to say to him.

They had finally agreed that he would take some time to process just seeing her again, and then maybe the three of them could meet for dinner and just talk. Ali wasn't sure what Wes thought *taking some time* meant, but she didn't want him to get totally wrapped up in this recent case and ignore Sara for the next year. In her mind, a few weeks was plenty of time.

She donned her scrubs and entered the autopsy room. She pulled out the body of Sam Porter from the locker and slid the corpse onto a gurney. As she prepared him for the autopsy, she focused in on her job. She loved this part of it. Hated the paperwork, but the autopsies—finding out the reason someone had died—that brought her joy.

She did the initial visual of the outside of his body before picking up the scalpel to begin the Y incision. Her movements were slow and precise as she cut open the body, then cut away the ribs. Once she exposed the organs, she removed them, placed them on a separate table, and began looking at each organ separately, taking samples and pictures of them. As she opened the stomach, the red, velvety appearance stopped her. She grabbed her camera and took pictures, recording her notes as she continued through each step.

By the time Ali finished the autopsy, she was exhausted. She carefully sewed up the incision on the body and pushed it back into the locker. The body wouldn't be able to be released for at least a few days. She needed to get ahold of Wes, and he would not like this.

The victim's wife accused Sara of killing Sam because he intended to break it off with her that night. She was very adamant that Sam had been afraid to cut ties, as she stated, "this girl, he realized, had a very vindictive streak and just wanted to get away from her." That had put Wes in a tough spot, wanting to—although mad at her—protect her at all costs. The autopsy would not look good for Sara.

Ali changed out of the scrubs and settled behind her desk. She quickly typed up the notes from the autopsy. She hit save and sat back. She dreaded the text to Wes, but she picked up her phone and typed a message:

Autopsy shows poison. Intentional by the amount of damage to the organs.

She continued through the day with paperwork, waiting to hear from Wes. Her conclusion for his silence was one of two options: he either had allowed his phone to go dead—which has happened before—or he was ignoring it, trying to figure out how Sara was tied to it.

She packed up early and was just getting all her things together when she heard a voice clear from the doorway. She turned slowly and found Wes grinning at her.

"Do you have a charger?" he meekly asked.

Ali shook her head in disbelief. "You have got to be kidding me."

Laughter bubbled out of Wes as he came toward her. "Yes. I remembered to charge my phone last night. I got your message."

Ali punched him in the arm. "And you didn't respond all day?"

Wes pulled her close and just held her for a moment. "It's been a long day."

"Fill me in." Ali moved back toward her chair, but Wes stopped her.

"Let's go for a walk. I could use some fresh air." Wes reached for her, and they strolled out of the morgue hand in hand.

They walked in silence for a couple of blocks and found themselves in Harris Park, a modest park with benches, a small field for kids to play ball, and some swings to the side with a slide. It was a great park for families with little children, but today it was empty, except for a couple of moms with their babies in strollers as they walked the perimeter of the park. Wes and Ali stopped at a bench off to the side and sat down.

Ali waited for Wes to talk. She had learned when she first met him that he talked on his own terms and always needed a few minutes to compose his thoughts when there was a big conversation coming. She watched the young moms and a wistful feeling tugged at her heart. Some day, she kept telling herself, some-day she would have her own child. She pulled herself out of her thoughts and turned toward Wes.

He was watching her. Her cheeks warmed and un-doubtedly pinked, but she smiled. "You ready to tell me about your day?"

He glanced toward the moms pushing the strollers, then back at Ali. He seemed puzzled, but Ali didn't say a word and just sat there, attentive to him. He cleared his throat. "I've been thinking about Sara and last night. I don't know what to think. She seemed gen-uinely upset when she talked about Sam being dead, but is she just a talented actress?"

Ali waited.

Wes rubbed his hand down his face as if to rub away any doubt he had. "I don't know, Ali. And now you're saying Sam was poisoned."

"Yes. Arsenic. What I couldn't tell is if it was a long-term exposure to it, or if it was one large dose."

"What would happen if it was over time?"

Ali thought for a moment. "Well, the stomach findings would be the same as far as color, etc. The nails would be pitted, and his weren't. He would have been having more GI distress at a lesser intensity. If I had to guess, I would say it was a onetime dosage. Which..." Ali paused, trying to soften her next words. "Which could mean that Sara gave it to him, and Sam was actually at her house longer than what she said, or someone poisoned him before he got to her house."

"Which means I need to figure out his steps before he arrived at her place," Wes concluded.

Ali smiled. He was stepping into a protective-brother role and trying to prove Sara innocent. She just hoped Sara didn't prove him wrong for believing in her.

four

Sara staggered from the bed as the knocking got increasingly louder, the longer she took to open the door.

She pulled it open to see her best friend, Evie, standing there. "What took you so long?" Evie asked as she pushed into the apartment. "You look like hell, girl."

Sara groaned. "Coffee?"

"Please."

"Fine. Wait until I tell you about last night!" Sara yelled from the kitchen as she brewed two cups of coffee. Thank God for a Keurig and the quickness of how she got her caffeine fix. She walked into the living room with the two mugs and handed one to Evie. Sara plopped down at one end of the couch.

"What happened?" Evie said, sitting on the other end. She glanced around. "What's that smell?"

Sara grimaced. "Vomit."

"Are you sick?" Evie eyed her.

Sara shook her head. "Sam was here last night. *He* was sick..." Repeating what happened tore her up. She took a sip of coffee to hide the emotion from Evie. "He didn't make it. I don't know if he had a heart attack or what, but I was told at the hospital that he had died."

Evie sat forward. "Are you kidding?"

"Why would I kid about that?" Sara snapped.

"Just an expression." Evie sat back, her free hand up in front of her, obviously warding off Sara's snippiness. "Do they know what caused it?"

"I don't know. No one at the hospital would tell me anything, and then his wife walked in with the police." Sara took a sip. "Worse yet, I ended up at the police station being questioned about it."

"What?" Evie put her mug down. "Are you okay? What could they possibly think you had done?"

Sara shook her head. "I don't know, and yes, I'm fine. I'm just exhausted, which is why I was still in bed when you got here."

Evie wrinkled her nose. "Well, let's clean. This smell is ruining my coffee for me."

Sara pointed at the trash can sitting by the kitchen doorway. "I rinsed it out, but I didn't have time to clean it."

"Enjoy your coffee. I've got it." Evie stood, grabbed the trash can, and headed to the bathroom. "Bleach in here?"

"Yes." Sara sat back. She was so thankful for Evie's friendship. They hit it off as soon as they had met each other. She felt like no matter what happened, Evie always had her back.

Sara drank her coffee and listened to the tub running as Evie washed the trash can. Sara stood to head to the kitchen to brew a second cup. While it brewed, she grabbed a couple of scented candles and lit them around the living room to dispel the lingering vomit smell.

Evie came back, smiling. "That's better."

Second cups in hand, they sat on the living room couch. They laughed and talked about Evie's escapades the night before on a date with a new man she had just met.

"Let's go out for brunch," Evie said.

"Okay. But give me ten minutes to shower and get presentable." Sara jumped up and ran to the bathroom.

They had no sooner stepped out Sara's door when her phone rang. She glanced at the number and didn't recognize it, so she pushed ignore. Linking elbows, she and Evie hurried down the stairs and onto the sidewalk. Sara's phone pinged with a text message.

"Someone really wants to get ahold of you," Evie commented.

Sara pulled the phone out of her pocket and saw the text:

It's Wes. We need to talk. Where can we meet?

Sara froze. She wasn't ready to sit down and talk with Wes. Could she get out of this or was it police business he was asking her to meet about? No, if it was police business, he would have told her to come to the station.

Not a good time. She hit send, silenced her phone, and slid it into her pocket. "Let's go."

Evie smiled. "I like your style. Where should we go?"

"The only place that has the best brunch in town," Sara replied, and they turned to cross the street.

Dawson paced the length of his workout room. *Why did Sara brush off my request to talk?*

He stopped walking and sent another text.

Still no response.

His fingers tightened around the phone. He closed his eyes and inhaled deeply to stave off the building steam. He made the first move, and she—once again—was deciding when he would talk to her. With a frustrated grunt, he dropped his phone on the bench next to his towel and moved to the punching bag. He wrapped his hands and pulled on his boxing gloves. The poor bag was going to feel the brunt of his frustration. An hour later, Dawson was still going strong, then his phone pinged with an incoming text message.

He paused and stared at the bag. Did Sara finally decide to respond? Well, *he* was unavailable now, and he resumed his punches. After a half-dozen hits, Dawson pulled off the gloves and wraps and picked up his phone. It hadn't been Sara. He'd gotten a text from Ali stating she was on her way over.

Dawson headed for the shower. He should have known Sara wouldn't reply. He couldn't tell if he was more irritated at her or at himself for being upset when this was typical of Sara's behavior over the past few years.

By the time Dawson dried off and got dressed, he could smell coffee brewing and knew that Ali had arrived. He smiled. Too bad she hadn't joined him in the shower instead of starting coffee. He stopped at the kitchen doorway and watched her as she busied herself with something he could not see. She had her back to him, and he just kept staring at her. He couldn't get enough of seeing her at ease in his house. She was humming when she turned around with two plates that had muffins on them.

She stopped and smiled. "How long have you been watching me?"

"Not long enough." He winked at her. "You could have joined me in the shower."

She grinned. "I could have, but then the muffins would have been cold, and well, I know how much you love them warm from the oven."

He moved around the table as she put the plates down. He pulled her close, she wrapped her arms around him, and their lips met. He broke the kiss off and looked down at her sweet face, smiling up at him. "Thank you," he said and cast his own smile.

"You're welcome." She gave him a quick hug, then turned and grabbed the coffee. "Sit."

He did as directed and waited for her to join him.

"Any word from Sara?" Ali asked as soon as she sat down.

He growled as he took a bite of the muffin.

"I take that as a no." Ali sat back with her coffee mug between her hands.

"I sent her a text asking her to meet. She responded with *not a good time*." He shrugged.

"I see."

Dawson looked up from his half-eaten muffin. "You see what?"

Ali laughed. "You are miffed because she brushed you off."

"I am not."

"Okay. I'm just surprised you wanted to talk to her so soon after reconnecting with her. I assumed you would want more time."

"Well, it's not just about us reconnecting. I have questions regarding Sam's death and her involvement."

"Ahh… there it is. So why not just ask her to the station?"

Dawson sat back. "I don't want to believe she has anything to do with this."

Ali reached for his hand. "Do you remember when we met with Cheryl Porter?"

"The psychic?"

21

"Yes. Do you remember her saying that Sara was going to need you, whether or not you wanted to help her? She said that you wouldn't be happy with her."

"Yeah. So, she got something right. She was guessing." Dawson scowled.

"Was she? Seems to me she fairly accurately predicted this exact scenario." Ali squeezed his hand. "I'm just saying I think Sara needs you, and she's afraid to ask for help because you aren't just her brother, you are a detective."

"I already know she's doing illegal business."

"Wes... you know no such thing. You assume it, but you don't know for sure. Why don't you hear her out and give her the benefit of the doubt?"

"It's not that easy," he softly said. "I can't just shut off the lawful side of me to be just a brother."

"What were you doing all those nights searching for her? You weren't searching for her because she had done something wrong. You searched because you love her. Don't let any new knowledge you *think* you have on her change that."

five

Dawson called Officer Brown to meet him at the station. He busied himself with looking over details of Samuel Porter. CEO of a finance company, married. No children. He was forty-five years old and apparently not in the best shape of his life. Dawson sat back and stared at the folder. Not much to go on. His wife was Cecilia Porter—a dutiful wife that spent her days attending charity events.

"Sir, you wanted to see me?" Brown came up behind Dawson.

Dawson stood and grabbed the folder. "Sure did. I need your help, and I already cleared it with your boss. You'll be helping me out in this case."

Brown grinned. "Happy to help."

Dawson nodded. "Let's go. I'll give you the details in the car."

As they drove to Sam Porter's office, Dawson sat in

the passenger seat and filled in Brown about the victim, the possible poison, and that they were looking for a coffee shop or coffee cart between his office and Sara Wesley's home where the victim had ended up. Dawson made a point to use Sara's chosen name instead of her given one. He didn't want anyone knowing that they were related as of yet.

Brown pulled into the parking lot of the finance office. They both exited the car and started for the door. "Let's begin with Mr. Porter's secretary or assistant, or whatever he had."

"Looks like Porter's office was on the fourth floor." Brown pointed at the signage next to the elevator.

Dawson pushed the elevator button. "Then that's where we start."

They rode the elevator in silence. The doors opened into a spacious waiting room, and Brown whistled under his breath. Directly across from the elevators was a long desk with hallways going off each side. They approached the desk to see a young woman working on a computer.

She smiled up at them. "May I help you?"

"Detective Dawson and Office Brown here to see Mr. Porter's assistant." Dawson flashed his badge at the girl.

"Pauline. She's down the hall to your right. Mr. Porter's office is the last one at the corner. Her office is right outside his." She went back to her computer, dismissing them.

Dawson started down the hall, knowing Brown followed right behind him. Abstract artwork covered the walls, pretty tastefully decorated, although it wasn't *Dawson's* taste. They arrived at the office, and he knocked on the open door before stepping in.

"Yes, how can I help you?" A middle-aged woman sat behind the desk. Her eyes looked red from crying, and she appeared a bit disheveled.

"I'm Detective Dawson. You're Pauline?"

"Yes, sir."

"I'm sorry to come in like this, but I have some questions regarding Mr. Porter that I am hoping you can answer."

"I just heard this morning." Pauline blew her nose again and dabbed at her eyes. "It seems impossible that he is gone."

Dawson nodded. "I'm so sorry for your loss."

Pauline glanced at Brown. "He was a good man."

Dawson smiled. "Can we look around his office?"

Pauline stood and opened the door to her left. The large office had windows across one full wall that looked out over the city. There was no clutter on the desk. In fact, the place was immaculate. Pauline followed Dawson and Brown into the office.

"There isn't much here," she said. "He took his laptop home with him every night. And of course, the office was cleaned that night after he left, so...." Her voice trailed off, and she sniffled.

"Can you tell me if he had anything to eat or drink that afternoon? I understand he was in the habit of having late-afternoon coffee."

Pauline nodded. "He was busy when his...*friend* showed up with a coffee for him. She left it with me."

"His friend?" Dawson glanced at her.

"Yes. I assume he sees her outside the office. I don't really know her, just have seen her face. He never calls her by name, and I don't ask. It isn't my place." Pauline bristled a bit.

"Could you describe her?" Dawson asked and noticed Brown had taken out his notebook and started scribbling something on the page.

"I honestly paid little attention to her. She would show up every so often and Sam had instructed me to always let her know he was busy. She would just pop in with coffee or muffins for him every now and then. She didn't come around all that much."

Dawson nodded. "But can you give us anything so we might be able to track her down to talk to her?"

Pauline glowered, staring into space. "Really, just one of those girls that blends into the background. Brownish hair, about my height...nothing really remarkable about her."

Dawson frowned. "Okay. Thank you, Pauline. If you think of anything else, please call me." He held out his card, and she took it.

Dawson tipped his head toward the door and Brown nodded. Dawson followed him into the hallway.

"Not much to go on, is it, sir?" Brown asked.

"Not at all." Dawson let out a frustrated huff. "Although we know someone brought him coffee that afternoon, and I would bet that's where the poison was. Unfortunately, without much of a description, it won't matter if we can find the coffee place it was bought since we can't ask about who bought it. Mostly a dead end. Let's go talk with the wife and see if she knows who the mystery girl was."

"You don't think it was the Sara person who you already questioned?" Brown asked.

"No, I don't." Dawson sighed. And he truly didn't think it was her. "She states he came to her place, but she hadn't seen him before he got there. I don't think she would go to his office to give him coffee if he was coming to her house."

Brown nodded. "Unless she's trying to throw us off."

"That's always a possibility. We won't completely rule her out, but let's go to the Porter's home and talk with the wife."

Dawson looked around as they pulled up to the large, sprawling house. The Porters obviously had some money, which would explain the ability for Sam to hire his sister. God, he hated even thinking of Sara being involved in that type of business, but he needed to put his personal feelings on the back burner and find a way to clear her name.

They exited the vehicle and as they started up the front steps, the door opened and a young man stood in the doorway.

Dawson pulled out his badge and held it up. "Detective Dawson, and this is Officer Brown. Is Mrs. Porter around?"

The man nodded. "She's been expecting someone to come by. Come on in."

Dawson turned to the young man as they entered the house. "And you are?"

The man held out his hand to initiate a handshake. "I'm Cecilia's nephew, Jason. I'm here for a few days to help her with the funeral preparations."

Dawson nodded. They followed Jason into a sparsely furnished, large living room. Cecilia Porter was sitting in an armchair facing a window.

"Aunt Cecilia, this is Detective Dawson and Officer Brown," Jason announced as they entered the room.

She stood and turned to face them. "Gentlemen, I was wondering when I would be visited by the police." She gestured to the couch and took another chair facing the couch as they sat down.

Dawson cleared his throat. "I'm sorry for your loss, Mrs. Porter." She nodded and he continued. "I understand Mr. Porter was CEO for Harpin Financial."

"Yes. He was extremely driven and worked long hours. Longer hours than he needed to."

Dawson slowly bobbed his head. "Can you tell me what his routine was typically?"

"He was up most mornings by five, at the office by six or six-thirty, and I would see him home about seven to eight at night. And that was unless he had some event going on, then it would be later."

Dawson sat back. "Did he have a lot of events going on?"

Cecilia crossed her legs. "Let me be frank, Detective. Events really means he was spending time with his mistress."

"And do you know this mistress?"

Cecilia laughed. "Detective Dawson, there have been many of them over the years. This newest one is a young thing. Her name is Sara something. She was at the hospital when I arrived to find my husband dead. I believe your men brought her to the station."

"Yes. With the statement you made that she had killed your husband. What can you tell me about that?"

"I believe it is pretty straightforward. She's been screwing my husband and probably was going to be thrown over for someone younger. I know he was on his way to break up with her."

"How do you know that? Is that something you talk about regularly with him?"

Mrs. Porter laughed. "A woman knows these things. And besides, Pauline keeps me appraised of what is going on."

"Pauline? Sam's assistant?"

"Yes. Have you met her?"

Dawson glanced at Brown. "Yes, ma'am. We just came from there. She stated she couldn't give us any information. She was very vague about things and certainly never mentioned she knew of other women."

Cecilia Porter shrugged. "I cannot say what she knows or doesn't know for sure. *I* know she has relayed to me a few things but has never given me names."

Dawson nodded. "Anything else you want to share with us? Did he have coffee regularly with anyone in the afternoons?"

"Not that I am aware of. I couldn't say who he had drinks with, coffee or otherwise."

Dawson stood, with Brown following. "If you think of anything else, please let us know."

"I want that bitch who killed him put away, Detective."

"I plan on finding out who did it and making sure justice is served." Dawson nodded.

"I handed her directly to you," Mrs. Porter snidely said. "Why has there not been an arrest?"

"There's no evidence that she was involved, Mrs. Porter. You state she did it, but did you witness it?"

Mrs. Porter scoffed. "Do your job, dear, and if you can't, I can make a call to find a detective who can."

Dawson met her eyes and held them. "There is not another detective who would arrest someone without any evidence. Have a good day, ma'am."

six

I sat outside the coffee shop, watching people go in and out. The place was always packed and I would go in sometimes just to watch the owner. He was engaged, but he had no problem with his eyes roaming. We had been an off-and-on thing for about a year now. Last week he told me he was no longer interested in keeping our arrangement. After further discussion, I found out that he was pursuing another woman.

The bastard. I could go to his fiancée, but what fun would that be? No, I would rather make him suffer a bit for the heartache he caused me. Now, I never thought he would leave his fiancée for me, but there had been enough talk about this being long term that it wasn't completely out of the realm of possibility.

I started walking from my car and went into the coffee shop. He looked up when I walked in.

"Medium hot coffee, black, please," I ordered.

Daniel turned to the coffee pot and filled my order. "On the house," he murmured as he handed it to me.

"You should join me," I suggested. He glanced over his shoulder toward the back room and shook his head. Ahh...the fiancée was there and he couldn't risk being seen with me. *Fine, we can play that game.*

I took my coffee and went to sit down by the window. He had put my coffee in a to-go cup instead of a mug, and I knew it irritated him when I decided to settle in at the table. I pulled a paperback from my purse and settled in to read while I drank my coffee. I kept an eye on him and when his fiancée left the shop, he moved his way toward me.

"What are you doing?" he demanded.

"Reading, drinking coffee..."

"Funny. Why here?"

I smiled. "It's the best coffee in town. Where did you think I would go? I'm not going to stop giving you my patronage just because you don't want to see me anymore. I'm not that childish."

He slid into the chair. "I'm really trying to work things out with Deb. I'm not trying to hurt you."

"You haven't. Would you prefer I take my business elsewhere?"

He sighed. "No."

"Okay, then. I'm just one of your customers. Nothing more, nothing less."

He stood and started to walk away. He turned back once, obviously thought better of it, and went back to the counter. I watched him go. The man was infuriating at times. *Work things out with Deb.* That was BS. I hated it when men lied to me. Did they not realize it was not the smartest move to make?

I sat back and finished my coffee while I watched him wait on customers. He would glance at me every so often, but his face was neutral.

Just before I stood to leave, his fiancée came walking back in. I eyed her, and when she glanced over to me, I smiled. She returned the smile and walked toward me.

"I've seen you in here before, haven't I?" she asked.

"Yes. It's the best coffee in town."

"Thank you. I'm Deb. This is my fiancé, Daniel, and my shop. We've been so blessed to have repeat customers like you."

"It's my pleasure. And congratulations on the engagement. When's the wedding?"

Deb smiled. "We're working on plans. I would love to do it this summer, but Daniel wants to wait a little bit. Says we need to make sure the coffee shop is financially sound before we get married."

I nodded. "Good advice, but then again, love shouldn't have to wait."

"I agree. It was a pleasure meeting you." Deb turned away and I looked at Daniel. He was watching me. A look of panic crossed his face before he glanced at his fiancée and smiled. I stood to leave, and with one more long deliberate look at Daniel, I walked out the door. I slipped my hand in my pocket and fingered the vial that was there. He would be a tricky one, but I'd make it happen, and then we'd see who would be left smiling. I just needed to make one particular phone call before Daniel took his final drink.

seven

Sara sat holding her phone and looking at the open text message from Wes. She debated how to reply. Her text of *not a good time* had been short, assuredly sending Wes into a tither thinking she was blowing him off again. She wanted that reconnection, but with this mess with Sam and his death at her house, and Wes being a cop, she didn't know how to go about it.

Could they reconnect without their individual jobs colliding? It seemed it was a little late for that. She sighed and started typing:

Can meet tomorrow if you're available.

She hit send and sat back on her couch. Relief washed over her as she realized how much she truly wanted to see Wes again. He had been her favorite sibling, and she'd missed him terribly through the years. Because she'd been keeping an eye on him the whole time, she knew he had been looking for her. He seemed to be doing so well in his career, even after being discharged from the military, and she didn't want to disrupt that.

She sat lost in her memories of Wes when they were kids—the way he used to tease her and she would get so mad at him. She smiled. She was still a bit hot-headed.

The ping of her phone interrupted her reminiscing.

10 AM at Brew's? Direct and to the point, just like Wes.

See you then, Sara replied, and then got up to get ready for an evening out. She had a feeling tonight was going to be a good night and maybe a start of something new. Evie had been pushing her to get out and do more. Because she went out so much for work, she enjoyed just staying in on evenings she had off. But she had agreed to meet this man, not for work, but for pleasure. Why shouldn't she have a bit of fun?

Sara stepped into the club and took everything in. It was crowded tonight and she hated this type of scene. Long ago, when she still lived in the Dawson home, she longed for this type of night out. She lived under a microscope with her parents always keeping their kids close. Her boyfriend had been her ticket out, and running away had been the best thing she had done. She didn't expect Wes to understand, but she had hoped he would at least listen to her. She mentally closeted any thoughts of her brother for the night and glanced around, looking for her *date*. She spotted him close to the bar, recognizing him from his profile picture. He caught her eye and waved her over.

"Sara, right?" he said.

"Yes, how are you?"

"I'm good, better now that you're here. I'm Sawyer." He looked down the length of her. "What are you drinking?"

"Cosmopolitan, please."

Sawyer ordered the drinks and turned to her as they waited. "Not my typical scene." He gestured around to the club.

"Mine either." Sara felt a wash of relief. "How about I grab that small couch in the back of the club where it might be a bit quieter to talk?"

He nodded, and she made her way to the couch. There were couches spread throughout the periphery of the club, with high-top tables scattered around the dance floor. At least they were away from the loudness of the music. Sawyer walked up and handed her the drink before he took the spot next to her. It didn't seem long and he was searching for a waitress to grab him another beer. After ordering another one, he sat back.

"I'm not looking for anything long term or serious." His statement came out of the blue, and Sara froze.

"Okay," she said. "What *are* you looking for?"

He leaned toward her. "I know the business you're in. I'm looking for companionship."

"I don't know what you heard, but I don't have that kind of business." She stood just as the waitress brought Sawyer his beer. He guzzled it down in two swigs and got to his feet, blocking her way.

"We both know you do. You came highly recommended."

"By whom?" Sara demanded.

"A friend."

"A friend of yours, but obviously not a friend of mine. Trust me, I don't offer what you're looking for." She sidestepped around him. "Night, Sawyer. Best of luck to you."

She glanced back as she made her way to the door. Just as she reached it, she saw out of the corner of her

37

eye, Sawyer holding his stomach. She slipped out the door and started home, walking with tears in her eyes. Every time she put herself out there personally, men just proved repeatedly what asses they were. Though professionally, didn't she see that all the time, too? The men who hired her were all married, or seriously involved, and yet they hired her behind their wives/ girlfriend's backs. What did that make her?

Maybe Wes was right, and she was just a glorified prostitute.

Sara woke up to her phone ringing. Twelve missed calls and two text messages, both from Wes asking her to call him ASAP. She put the phone down and turned over in bed. She didn't want to deal with her brother at the moment. The phone immediately rang again, and she picked it up.

"What?"

"You need to get to the station *now*." Wes's voice was low, yet intense. "I can't help you if you don't get here."

"Help me with what?"

"God, Sara. There is another man you know that was found dead last night."

Sara sat up in bed. "What? Who?"

"Get here and we'll talk. If you are not here in the next thirty minutes, they will send an officer to get you and that will look worse for you."

"I'm on my way."

Sara dressed and hurried out the door. Who was the man? She wasn't even with anyone last night. She had taken a night off, which she hadn't done in a long, long time. She thought back to the previous night and remembered leaving the club and vaguely looking back to see Sawyer doubled over, holding his stomach.

Oh, God, it can't be him.

That was the first time she had met him.

Sara arrived at the station within twenty minutes,

and Wes was waiting for her. He took her into an interrogation room. He motioned for her to sit down and waited until she sat before he took the seat across from her.

"Where were you last night? Working?" he asked without any hesitation.

"Actually, I wasn't working. I met a blind date at a club, and then left because I found him to be a jerk."

Wes sat back. "Who was it?"

"His name was Sawyer. He showed his true colors immediately. I didn't even finish a drink before I left."

"What was he doing when you left?"

Sara narrowed her eyes at her brother. "Having another drink. Why?"

"The dead man that we have is Daniel Sawyer. He dropped dead at a club last night and witnesses state they saw you walking away from him right before he died."

"Shit. I don't know a *Daniel* Sawyer, but the guy said his name was Sawyer." Sara sat back and closed her eyes. "What the fuck, Wes? You don't think *I'm* responsible, do you?"

"I'd like to believe you aren't, but come on, Sara... it's not like we have been in close contact all these years. I don't know you anymore."

"That doesn't make me a killer. You know that deep down."

Wes sighed. "I want to believe in you, but I have to be objective and do my job. Understand?"

She huffed. "I suppose."

"Where did you meet this Sawyer?"

Sara frowned. "Dating app called CupidSwan."

Wes stared at her. "You're on a dating app?"

"Why does that seem so hard to believe?" Sara demanded.

"Seriously? You go out with men for business, and then you want to *date* someone?"

Sara's eyes teared. "You think I enjoy going out with men for work, and then always being alone? I would much rather find someone to have in my life that I know just loves me and is not using me."

Wes nodded. "Okay. So, you never met this Sawyer before last night?"

Sara shook her head.

"Stay put." He got up and left the room.

Dawson stood in the hallway and leaned against the door upon closing it. He tried to think through what he knew so far. Both victims had been with Sara either at the time of, or right before, their deaths. It wasn't evidence of her involvement, but it certainly didn't look good for her. He knew his sister wasn't a murderer, yet someone really wanted him to think she was.

His thoughts drifted back to his meeting with Cheryl Porter in his last case. He didn't believe in psychic ability, yet she had been right on the money as far as Sara needing him. Did he call her in and get her opinion? He smirked. His boss would have a field day with that after Dawson had given him such a hard time over talking with her before.

Sara was full of surprises. He didn't expect her to want to actually have a relationship with someone. Maybe the escort job, hopefully, was not fulfilling for her, so she wanted to find a way to get out of it.

He pulled aside one of the young cops walking by. "Can you get me some information on some dating app called CupidSwan?"

"Yes, sir." Before Dawson could finish rolling his eyes, the rookie was gone.

Dawson moved to the bullpen and his desk and

started flipping through contacts on his phone. He came to Cheryl Porter, the psychic, and he paused. He trusted intuition more than anything in his job, especially when it was early in an investigation. His gut had never been wrong, and he hoped it would prove him right again, despite his doubts.

He pushed the call button and listened to the ringing coming through.

"Detective Dawson, what a surprise," Cheryl answered on the third ring.

Dawson laughed. "Is it really? I thought you would have known I'd be calling."

"Oh, I knew I would hear from you. I just expected you to fight it a bit longer."

"Fair enough." Dawson smiled despite himself. He may doubt the so-called psychic ability, but at least Cheryl was pleasant to talk to.

"I believe you have reconnected with you sister, although under questionable circumstances." Cheryl jumped right in.

"Yes. How did you know that was going to happen when we first met?"

"Still doubting, I see." Cheryl paused as if waiting for him to say something, but he kept his mouth shut. "I get it," she went on. "There are a lot of skeptics out there, but I believe deep down you don't truly doubt what you can't see."

"Honestly, not sure what I believe. But I am hoping you can help me, or at least provide a brief insight however you do it. Would it be possible for you to come to the station? I'd like you to meet Sara and maybe see what your thoughts are?"

"I'd be honored, Detective. When were you thinking?"

"Would now be too soon?" Dawson asked.

"I'll be there within the half hour." Cheryl hung up without another word and Dawson couldn't help but respect her bluntness. He hated endless chatter just to fill space.

He stood and headed back to Sara. There were still things they could talk about before Cheryl got there.

As before, Sara stood looking out the window with her back to the door when Dawson walked in. She didn't turn. He stood and just watched her for a second. Her shoulders were slumped as if in defeat, and he wondered if it was because she was guilty and now caught, or if she was just defeated by the fact that someone would set her up like this? He hoped for the latter. He wanted to believe that his sister—the one that would tease him endlessly and who was always there for him when he was younger—was still in there.

He *had* missed her, but he didn't realize just how much until she was right there in front of him. Torn between wanting to strangle her for never getting in touch, and just wanting to pull her into a hug and hold on tight to her, he was in an impossible situation with the investigation going on with her in the middle of it.

"What's the word?"

Dawson startled at the sound of Sara's voice and found that she had turned around and faced him.

He smiled. "Nothing yet, but let's talk some more."

She came back to the table and sat down. Dawson and she held gazes for a moment before he dropped his eyes to his notebook.

"Wes," she said softly.

He looked back up. "It's okay. We'll figure it out."

That was it. There was no need to say anything more about the past for now. He knew in that moment his sister was innocent and he would go through hell to make sure she was removed from any suspect list. "Okay. This isn't going to be a pleasant subject for either of us, but we need to talk about the business and your clients."

She nodded. "What do you want to know?"

"Tell me how this started. I know you don't want to name clients, but it might be important to know who you are involved with."

She grimaced with a slight shake of her head in protest, and then stopped. "You are not going to want to hear this, Wes."

"Trust me, I don't want to, but I'm not here as your brother right now. I'm here to solve the crime."

She took a deep breath and exhaled slowly. "It started when I ran away from home. I know Mom and Dad were furious with me. They didn't want me hanging out with Rick. I just needed to be free from the controlling atmosphere." She stood and walked over to the window. "Rick didn't have the money saved for us to go like he said he did. We were drinking one night—well, I was drinking apparently. I thought we both were, but he was plying me with drinks to the point where I didn't really know what was going on."

Sara glanced at Dawson. She turned to face him and leaned against the wall. "He had lined up some friend of his to come in. I didn't know what I was doing...I was drunk." She closed her eyes as if trying to block out the memory. "He pimped me out, Wes."

Dawson swore under his breath but remained calm. His hands clenched and unclenched. "How many times?"

"I honestly don't know. Too many to count. I didn't realize it at first because every time, he would get me drunk so I didn't really remember what was going on, but suddenly he had money and wasn't working. When I confronted him about it, he filled me in on *my part* of it. When he went out that night, I searched our place and found the stash of money. I took most of it and left."

"How does that lead into your business now?" Dawson quietly asked.

Sara came back to the table and sat down. "I was a prostitute, Wes. He made me one. But I didn't want to live that life. I tried waitressing for a while, but I couldn't make any money...not enough to live on. I didn't have a college education and couldn't afford to go to college." She sighed. "I met this girl in the course of waitressing, and she asked if I wanted to work for her. Deep down, I knew it was probably back to prostitution, but she assured me it wasn't."

Dawson sat back and waited for Sara to calm herself. She was visibly shaken while talking about her past. He watched her eyes as they filled with tears. Her hands shook, so she clasped them together. All signs that telling her history wasn't easy for her and definitely not some fictitious story she was trying to sell. Honesty was good, no matter how hard it was for him to listen to it.

"She ran an escort business," Sara continued. "She bought me nice clothes and said her clientele was high-end, businessmen. There was no expectation for sex. Most of the men truly wanted someone they could go out with. Most of them wanted sex, but it was my prerogative to say yes or no. We set my boundaries and for a while, I was hired to escort men who came in from out of town to business dinners and stuff like that. I realized I was making less than the other girls because I said no to sex. The woman who ran the operation came to me and was honest again, stating I was in high demand, but they wanted sex. I didn't want to be a prostitute, but I needed to get into a nice neighborhood to live. I was scared to death where I was living that I would run into Rick. I didn't want to risk that. So, I agreed to take on just one or two who wanted sex...just until I could move."

Dawson closed his eyes. No wonder she didn't want to contact him. She was selling herself, and he was a cop. He grimaced and opened his eyes to look at her. Tears were running down her cheeks now, and it broke his heart. "Sara, did you ever think that you could contact me and I could help you?"

She shook her head. "I knew you would be ashamed of me. Wes, I failed you in so many ways. I no longer was a sister you could look up to, and I didn't want my poor decisions to interfere with your job."

"Sara, I'm not ashamed. I had no idea all that was going on. I would have helped you, and damn if I don't want to find that asshole who started all this now."

Sara smiled through her tears. "He's not worth it. Besides, I heard he overdosed last year. Not sure if it's true or not, but if it is, he got what he deserved."

"So how did working for this woman—who you will not name—turn into your own business?"

"Actually, she was killed in a car accident. Hit by a drunk driver. Regardless of the business, she was good to me when I needed someone. After that happened, the other girls that worked for her dispersed, going to look for other work." Sara looked as if she was struggling to find her words and twisted her fingers into knots. "I shouldn't have, but I went through her things before her family got there to clean them out. I found her records of her clients and their contact information, their likes, dislikes, etc. She even had what they would pay for what, and it was a lot more than she ever paid us. She was making a lot off the girls she hired. So, I took her records. I weeded through them and contacted the ones that didn't expect sex. I told them I would honor the same prices for them, and my business was started. Over the years, I have had others approach me on recommendations from some of my clients. Very few of them I actually have sex with, but occasionally, there are a few special ones who have been long-term customers that I will do that for."

She sighed as she finished her story. Dawson nodded. It wasn't the greatest business, but at least she wasn't completely prostituting herself.

"I don't charge them extra for the sex," she earnestly added. "I have sex with them because I want to, Wes. It's not prostitution."

Dawson leaned forward. "Are you trying to convince me or yourself, Sara?"

She cocked her head at him, and then shrugged.

eight

There was a knock on the door, and Dawson glanced over as it opened. "Sir, a Ms. Porter is here to see you."

Dawson nodded and turned to Sara. "Hang tight. I'll be right back."

He left the room to find Cheryl leaning against the wall just down the hall from the interrogation room. She smiled and straightened when she saw him. "It's been going well with your sister." She made the statement as if she had been witnessing their interaction.

Dawson rolled his eyes. "I don't know why you keep trying to convince me."

"I'm not trying to convince you. Just pointing out the obvious. At some point you will come to the realization of what is the truth."

He shook his head. "Ever the cryptic." He gestured for her to follow him. "I'm not sure what I'm looking for, but I'm hoping to gain some insight into what is going on."

He opened the door and allowed Cheryl to precede him into the room. He watched Sara's reaction to the new arrival, but she just sat there watching.

"Hi, Sara." Cheryl broke the ice.

"Hi. Do I know you?" Sara replied.

"No, you don't. But I know you, sort of. I work with your brother on murder cases to try and give him some unseen clarification."

Sara scoffed. "My brother doesn't believe in psychics."

"Tell me something I don't know." Cheryl laughed.

"Very cute, you two. Let's get down to business." Dawson sat next to Sara while Cheryl took the seat across from her.

Sara sat forward. "Well, I'm curious. What do you know of me and these men who I supposedly murdered?"

Cheryl looked at her, and then at Dawson. "You two are a lot alike." She turned back to Sara. "I know you didn't do it, but I also know you are integrally woven into the circumstances."

"Well, I don't even know how I'm involved in this, so you know more than I do."

Dawson flipped open the file. "Look. What we know right now is the first victim died at Sara's place, and the second victim, just after she left. Other than that, there doesn't seem to be any connection between the two men, and only one of them was one of Sara's, um... *clients*. We're looking into the dating app that Sara was on, but right now, we've got nothing to go on."

"Who would want to make your life miserable?" Cheryl asked. "Because there is someone that has a very deep hatred for you."

Sara sat back. "I don't know anyone that would want to hurt me. I'm unaware of any enemies."

Dawson tapped his pen on his pad of paper. "Any former colleagues of yours that might have found out you have all the records from their previous employment?"

"Not that I'm aware of. I certainly haven't been in touch with any of them since her death." Sara started twirling her hair around her finger—a signature move she made when she was upset. Dawson inwardly smiled. It was good to know that the old Sara was still there.

Dawson faced her directly. "How did you meet the first victim?"

"He was a client with my former employer. I had accompanied him numerous times when I worked for her. He was one I contacted for continued service."

"I know you don't want to say, Sara, but it might be relevant for us to know who your former employer was. It's not going to hurt her as she is gone."

Sara frowned. "Some of these clients, though, still want their privacy."

"I'm not looking for their names right now. I'm looking for her name only. Maybe this is related to her. Could this Sawyer, or Daniel Sawyer, been a client of hers?"

Sara's brows drew together. "I honestly don't know. I don't remember seeing his name anywhere. I could go back through her records. I still have everything. I had never seen him before I met him last night."

"And last night was not a business meeting," Cheryl broke in. "Was it?"

Sara glanced at Dawson. "No. It was a personal first date."

He sat back in frustration. "We've got nothing to go on. Other than you being there, nothing to really connect you to this latest person. I am not even sure the deaths *are* connected. I'll wait to hear what Ali says after she does an autopsy."

"Can I go then?" Sara asked.

Dawson nodded. "I'll need those records of your former employer though. I want to be able to double-check names myself."

"Guess there's no need for that coffee now." Sara gave him a half smile.

Dawson pulled out his phone, typed out a quick text, and hit send. Sara's phone pinged and she peeked at it. Of course, he knew what it said: *Dinner tonight my place 6 pm.* She nodded before standing up and leaving.

Dawson noticed that Cheryl had been watching him from across the table. "They *are* connected," she said.

"The deaths?" he asked.

"Yes. You know it in your gut, just as you know Sara isn't involved."

"What can you actually tell me that is something new?" Dawson snarked.

Cheryl smiled and stood up. "I'll be in touch, detective. Keep an open mind."

nine

Sara hadn't been home long when she dove into the records of her former employer. Maybe it had been wrong to obtain them by stealing them, but the woman was dead, and what was her family going to do with them anyway? Madame hadn't liked anything digital, so there were multiple ledgers and notebooks with different information. Ledgers had all the transactions ever done with codes for the clients. Another notebook kept all the clients with their transaction codes, along with their likes and dislikes, which escorts they preferred—also coded by their escort names—as well as any dirt she had found on them...*Just in case she ever needed it* she would say. There was also a notebook for men who wanted to be clients, but were not, and the reason they were denied.

Sara sat on the floor of the living room and spread

out the various ledgers and notebooks around her. She made piles of the ledgers with the most recent on top, another pile for the notebooks of clients, and the one notebook of wannabe's. She reached for her laptop and opened it beside her, pulling up a spreadsheet so she could make some notes.

She started with the notebook of clients, scanned through it, and saw Sam's name. He had a lot of likes and dislikes, and in fact, was quite particular when it came to some things. Funny, he had said little about his particulars when he started with Sara. She frowned as she saw a note underneath in smaller print, noting that he could be quite deviant. That was a side of him she had never seen, and he had been her client for years. She flipped open the ledger that held the last two years of the business. These particular ledgers were big and heavy.

She pulled her laptop closer and started tallying up the amount of money Sam had spent while with Madame. He had been with her for three years and spent well over a hundred thousand with her. Sara knew he had money but hadn't realized just how much. She sat back and reflected on what little she really had known of him. He had been with her once or twice, never sexually when she worked for Madame. As she looked through notes, she was seeing he had quite the predilection for one girl in particular, and she had been noted for taking on the *kinky* guys.

So, why continue to work with me when that stuff was never part of the deal?

Maybe he was also paying someone else to fulfill that side of him. She shrugged. It really didn't matter anymore. He was gone and with him a good chunk of her income.

She pushed the ledger aside and started looking back through the notebook of clients, searching for

Daniel Sawyer. She didn't remember his name, but then again, he wasn't the one she had taken on. He still could have been a past client. She went through all the notebooks of clients without locating him. She then moved on to the notebook of wannabes. There he was at the top of the list. He had applied two weeks before Madame's car accident. She had denied him based on lack of income. *Interesting.* He certainly hadn't dressed like someone who had an income to burn, which was apparently one requirement to be a client. There were no other notes on him.

Sara pulled her laptop onto her legs and started a search for Daniel Sawyer. He owned a coffee shop. He had only told her he was a business owner. Okay. Not really a lie. She certainly hadn't told him what she did, although he knew, and that tidbit bothered her more than anything. She found he was also engaged. Other than that, nothing else. He was a nobody in the world. How had he found out what she did? She glanced at her watch and realized she needed to get ready if she was going to get to Wes's on time for dinner.

Sara pulled into Wes's driveway. She shut off the car and just sat there for a moment. How many nights had she left notes and stood in the shadows, aching to talk to her little brother? Stifling the urge to run to him and hug him close?

She sighed.

She had made so many mistakes in her years since she left home. Her biggest regret was cutting Wes out of her life. She closed her eyes, imagining their young days. Wes was her biggest champion and, truth be told, had been her best friend. It had killed her to leave him behind, but Rick had insisted they not tell him anything. Looking back, she could see the manipulation that Rick had done in her life, alienating her from her family. And Sara had been too young and starry-eyed to see beyond the hope of getting out from under her parents' control.

She startled at the knock on her window and Wes opening her door. "Are you coming in?"

"Yes. Just got lost in memories, I guess." Sara stepped out of the car.

Wes pulled her into a hug. "I'm sorry it has been these circumstances that have brought you back into my life, but I'm glad you're here."

"Me, too," Sara whispered, tears welling up in her eyes. She hadn't been prepared for the emotions that washed over her with this contact from Wes. She had tried so hard to harden her heart when it came to the longing of being in contact with her brother, with someone so familiar that knew her inside and out. He gave her a small squeeze before he pulled away.

"Come on. Ali's been cooking up a storm. She's thrilled it isn't just me eating all the food for a change. I didn't realize how much she liked to host company." Wes cringed.

Sara laughed. That was just like him—teasing about the people he loved the most. "I'm glad you have her."

They walked into the kitchen, and Sara's senses overloaded. The yeasty scent filled her nostrils as she was transported back to being a kid and working with her grandmother in the kitchen. Gram had always made homemade bread, and it had been Sara's favorite. She came back to the present when she heard the snort behind her as Wes tried to hide his laughter.

"Yup, that smell." He grinned as he pulled out a seat for her at the table. "Want a drink?"

"Whatever you're having." Sara glanced around. "Nice house."

"Thanks." Wes set down a bottle of beer in front of her. "Rather have wine?"

Sara wrinkled her nose. "Absolutely wine. I didn't think you still drank that sludge."

"Still? I was sixteen when you left. How do you know what I drink?" Wes pulled out a bottle of red wine from the counter. "I opened it earlier to let it breathe." He poured a glass and put it in front of her.

"Okay. I've seen you drinking every so often." She took a sip. "You know, I almost ran into you at a restaurant just a little while ago. You stopped to talk to my date while I was in the bathroom."

Wes eyed her. "Date?"

"Don't, Wes. I want to be able to talk with you without the judgment every time I mention my job, or a date, or whatever. Please, Wes, I beg you just let it go."

"Fair enough. I'm sorry." He turned to Ali. "How much longer?"

"It would get on the table a lot faster if you would grab some of this food instead of just sitting on your ass."

Wes mocked surrender and jumped up to help. Once food was on the table and plates were filled, the atmosphere relaxed. Sara and Ali had a lively discussion around Ali's job and what kind of things she saw at the morgue.

"Who was the psychic that you brought in today?" Sara asked Wes to bring him back into the conversation.

Ali's eyes widened. "You called Cheryl?"

Wes nodded, then looked at Sara. "Cheryl is the psychic who helped us on my last murder case. Quite a dark one."

"I must say I was a little shocked to see her there... knowing your skepticism," Sara said and turned to Ali. "Obviously you're shocked by it, too."

"To be honest, I'm rarely shocked by your brother's actions anymore. He likes to think he's all mysterious, but he's not."

"I'm sitting right here." Wes pointed to himself and stood. "Another drink anyone?"

Sara and Ali both chimed in their affirmatives. Wes grabbed a couple of beers and refilled Sara's wine glass.

"Was this a social invite, little brother, or was this to continue the interrogation?" Sara smiled.

Wes mocked stabbing himself with a knife. "It was an invitation to my sister, who I haven't seen in years. Nothing more, nothing less."

Sara cocked her head at him. "Then you don't want to know what I found while I was searching through past client records?"

"Spill. But for the record, this is not the reason I invited you over."

Sara sat back as both Ali and Wes leaned forward. She grinned at the two. They were made for each other. "Sam was a longtime client even before I went on my own. What I didn't know was that Sawyer, or Daniel—whatever his name is—was someone who had applied to be a client and was denied."

"Did you know him before?" Wes asked.

"Never heard of him or seen him before he popped up on the dating app." Sara shrugged. "Do you think he specifically targeted me?"

"I don't know, but I can't say that there isn't a connection. You said he mentioned your business?"

"Yes. That's when I left."

Ali tapped her fingers on the table. "I did the autopsy today. It was the same as Sam's...arsenic. A lethal dose, I think, as opposed to smaller quantities that would take time."

"How much does it take to kill someone like that?" Sara asked, and Wes scowled at her.

"It would have to be three grams or more," Ali replied. "Maybe a little more to have it act so quickly. Which really is only about a teaspoon...easily mixed into food or drink without it being noticed."

"Sam usually drank coffee in the late afternoon, especially if he had a late night coming up. He would have gotten it at the office or on the way to see me. And at the club, Sawyer had a couple of beers."

Wes stood and started clearing the dirty dishes from the table. "The question becomes, who put it in their drink. We are talking two very different venues and there is no way of knowing where Sam got the coffee. I could ask at his office if he had made coffee before he left, but if he didn't, there could be any number of places he could have gotten it."

ten

Dawson had texted Brown to meet him at Brew House. The local coffee shop had been opened for a few years, and ironically, it was owned by the second victim: Daniel Sawyer. Dawson ordered coffee and sat down at a table off to the side where he could see the door and the counter, and just take it all in. Brown arrived within minutes of Dawson settling in. After ordering a coffee, Brown joined him.

"Have you been here before?" Brown asked. "This coffee is the best around. They roast their own beans using various flavors. The cinnamon roast is amazing." He inhaled the scent of the coffee.

Dawson did the same before taking a sip. It was good. "I didn't know you were such a connoisseur of coffee."

Brown grinned. "I dabble and have researched it a lot. I have tried a bit of home-roasting, but it definitely isn't close to being this good."

"Glad we could find a place you liked." Dawson snickered. "The real reason we are here, though, is that our second victim was the owner of this establishment. I want to talk to his fiancée, and when I called her, she said she would meet us here as she needed to keep the place open."

Brown nodded. They sat in silence, enjoying the coffee. Brown sat with his back to the counter but kept watching the door and out the window. Dawson watched both the counter and the door. The place was bustling. The two girls behind the counter were busy with orders. After about an hour, the place started to quiet to a steady stream of customers, but nothing overwhelming. A young woman stepped out of the back and came around the counter, heading toward their table.

"Detective Dawson, I'm so sorry to keep you waiting."

He stood and pulled the extra chair out for her. "No worries. This place is hopping in the morning."

She smiled. "Yes, we certainly are fortunate that it has taken off. I'm hoping I can maintain it with Daniel gone."

Dawson sat when she did. "Ms. Walker, this is Officer Brown."

"Ma'am, pleasure to meet you. This has been a favorite place of mine since you opened." Brown blushed.

"Thank you, sir. I hope we continue to see you, and please call me Deb." Deb smiled at Brown, then turned her attention back to Dawson. "What do you need from me?"

Dawson casually sat back in the chair. He rotated his coffee mug in his hands as he watched her. "Can you tell me why Daniel was in the club the night he died?"

Deb frowned. "I'm not sure. I didn't know he was

going to the club. He simply stated he was meeting up with a friend to catch up before he got hitched."

"I see. And you had no reason to doubt that?" Dawson asked.

"No reason at all. Daniel has always been faithful to me."

Dawson hated this part of the job. He never wanted to taint the way someone remembered a loved one, but he knew this particular victim was out looking for a quick lay at the very least, if not more of a consistent agreement with Sara's business. He decided to play it dumb. "We were told that he was seen with a female, then may have had a disagreement, and she left. Would you know anything about that?"

Deb shook her head. "Nothing. I mean girls flirted with Daniel here all the time. But he never was anything more than friendly with them. Do you think it was someone who was trying to pick him up, and he rejected her?"

Dawson slowly nodded. "I suppose that could be a possibility. From what I know when I spoke with her though, she was meeting him for a blind date and had met him on a dating app."

Deb sat back in her chair and stared at Dawson. "I don't know what to say to that. Do you have his phone? I know his passcode and get into it. He didn't believe in hiding things. He gave me his passcode, and because he was so upfront with it, I didn't feel there was any need to doubt him."

"The phone is probably at the morgue with his belongings. An autopsy was done immediately. I'm sure you can get the belongings." Dawson glanced at Brown.

Brown nodded. "I'll call Dr. Jensen, sir, and see if they can be picked up." He stood and left the table to make the call.

Dawson turned back to Deb. "I know that it's hard to hear this stuff, but in order to have the best chance at catching his killer, I need to know what he was doing, and with who. This isn't going to be pleasant if he truly was having an affair."

She nodded. "I know." Tears filled her eyes and threatened to spill over, but she blinked them away. "I'll do whatever I can to help. Trust me, I don't wish him dead, but I'm glad to have found this out before we married."

Brown returned. "You can pick up his personal things anytime at the County Morgue, ma'am. Dr. Ali Jensen will be your contact person."

"Thank you, sir." Deb stood. "I'm sorry, but I really need to get back to work. I'll call you, Detective, once I get his phone and get into it. I hope I find nothing, but trust me, you will be the first to know what I find."

Dawson rose to his feet. "Of course. I'll wait to hear from you."

eleven

I paced my living room, irritation running over me with every step. I needed to ramp up my game if I wanted to win. I stopped short and wracked my brain for the perfect outcome. I could see the business becoming busier and busier if I could just get the *obstacle* out of the way. This just wasn't going as I had intended...but when did life ever go the way I planned? Everything I did I always seemed to be in the shadow, never pushing past the leaders and always being second best. I was furious at the thought that I still was not on top yet.

I had poured through records and had been recruiting. I was going to start my own business. Women had been running escort businesses for years and there were more than enough men willing to pay for a companion for the evening. I had known different types of escort businesses, ones that ran from providing just a companion to social outings, to ones that prostituted out their escorts. I was open to doing whatever it took to make the money that would put me in the lifestyle I wanted.

I picked up the newspaper. Not much said about the second victim. I sighed. How can someone get any recognition for taking out the trash when the public didn't know about it? I grunted and sat down at the table, then pulled my box to me and opened it. All the wedding rings just waiting for the perfect man. Maybe I was thinking about this the wrong way. Maybe I didn't need a husband, just the business I wanted where all the men wanted me and I didn't have to make a choice. I had never wanted a husband, yet in the back of mind, a memory from somewhere remained that I needed a husband to get out of this hell of a home. Not sure where those thoughts came from since I had been living on the street for as long as I could remember. I ran away when I was twelve.

Refocusing my thoughts, I picked up two vials of the prepared arsenic and pocketed them. It was time to up the ante. I grabbed my dark-blue scarf, wrapped it around my head, and added my sunglasses. I wasn't trying to be incognito, but I didn't need to stand out, either. There was a sale going on at Mercier Motors. Maybe what I needed was a new yellow convertible.

I walked into the dealership and looked around. It bustled with people. All salesmen were apparently helping customers. No one approached me when I walked in and that suited me just fine. I walked over to the nearest SUV on the showroom floor and pretended to read the list of accessories that it held. It was a cute little thing, though not my style. I preferred a convertible, yellow, that would have me standing out and everyone looking at me as I drove by.

I moved on to another vehicle that wasn't too crowded with people. From this viewpoint, I could see into the owner's office. Salesmen were in and out, looking to close deals. I saw him sitting behind the desk, all important and whatnot. I rolled my eyes behind my sunglasses and frowned. This could have been a man that would have fit right into my plan. A big spender, and a man who was easy on the eyes. However, his first question was about who worked with me, obviously pushing me to the side as an option to keep him company.

"Can I help you find something, miss?" A young man stood to my left, waiting expectantly for an answer.

I smiled. "What do you have in a yellow convertible?"

"We have a brand new one that just came in. All the bells and whistles."

I glanced past him to the manager's office. "Sounds expensive. You better have the big boys ready to make the deal."

The young man paused for a second, and then grinned. "Think I'm not big enough, huh?"

"It will be like taking candy from a child." I gestured around me. "Lead the way."

The salesman became a running commentary on all the frills of the car, how great I would look in it, and any other compliment he obviously thought was necessary to keep my interest.

"I'd take it for a drive," I said, "but I forgot my license at home."

He looked around. "I won't tell. I'll say I'm driving it."

I nodded. He was hungry for a sale. Poor kid probably hadn't been able to get in the deep end with all the experienced salesman working today. When we got back from the test drive, I decided to put him out of his misery. "I'll take it."

The excitement oozed from him and he acted like

he could hardly keep himself from doing a victory dance. "Right this way."

"I want ten grand knocked off the top of it," I stated as soon as I sat down at his desk. Poor thing, he looked panicked. "Why don't you go talk to your manager, and I'll wait."

He hurried away from his desk and into the manager's office. The manager peeked out the door while talking to him. The young salesman soon came back and asked me to join him in the manager's office. I smiled. *Like taking candy from a baby.*

"Miss?" He stuck out his hand to shake mine. I shook his hand, ignoring the question in his voice. "I'm Philip, owner here."

"Can you make it happen?" I asked in a clipped tone. I needed to get the salesman out of the office.

"We can see what we can work out. Derrick tells me you want ten grand off the price."

"We both know that is the suggested retail price, and taking ten grand off is not going to kill your profit." I looked at my nails, bored with the whole conversation.

I could feel Philip's eyes on me as he watched me. "Will you be looking to finance?"

"Yes, but not a penny more than what I am asking the price to be." I looked up at him. My sunglasses shielded my eyes, but I saw the question when he thought he recognized me.

He started his Keurig behind his desk. "Can I get you a cup of coffee?"

"No, thank you. I'm on a bit of a time crunch, so let's make this happen."

He nodded. "Let me talk with my finance guy and see what we can do." I watched him walk out the door and down the hall. I walked quickly to the Keurig that was still brewing and emptied a vial into his coffee, watched it dissolve to make sure there would be no clumps, and then sat back down.

Philip came in and cleared his throat. He grabbed the coffee mug and took a sip. "Unfortunately, we just can't do the ten grand. How about we meet in the middle at five?"

"I don't need the car. I'll wait. Thank you so much for your time." I stood and nodded to him before walking out. I glanced for the young salesman who I had talked with before and saw him with another couple. Hopefully, he would forget I was even there. Philip wouldn't be talking to anyone about me, that was for sure.

I took one more look back at Philip and found him watching me as he sipped his coffee.

twelve

Dawson couldn't believe that less than a week had gone by and another body had shown up. He received a call from the hospital when a man was brought in unresponsive and had died shortly after arrival. The wife had not been with him, as she was taking her husband's place at their car dealership, and apparently, the sale going on was much more important than her husband's dropping dead. Dawson walked into the ER of the hospital.

"I'm looking for Dr. Davison." He held up his badge and waited while the doctor was paged.

"Detective Dawson." A young man in a white coat held out his hand. "I'm Dr. Davison...Grant Davison."

Dawson shook his hand. "Nice to meet you."

The doctor gestured for Dawson to follow him, and as they passed through the doors leading to the doctor/patient area, Dr. Davison cleared his throat. "I had heard about the murders with arsenic, and this death seems a bit suspicious to me. I'm fairly new here and the higher ups feel that it was just a heart attack, but we won't know that until there is an autopsy."

"And when will that be?" Dawson asked.

"Waiting on the wife's agreement, but she didn't come to the hospital"

"Where was he when the body was found?"

"My understanding is that he dropped in his office. He owns Mercier Motors."

Dawson turned toward him. "What do you mean dropped?"

"That was it. He didn't drop holding his chest. According to the EMT, they were told he was holding his stomach and had started to vomit."

"We need that autopsy ASAP," Dawson said and turned toward the door. "I need to get to that dealership. I'll be in touch."

Once in his car, he drove in the direction of the dealership, while dictating a text to Ali. *Possibly another one. Get in touch with Dr. Davison at the hospital.*

He arrived at the dealership in record time. He was shocked at the number of people around, in and out of the place. As he entered, he was approached by a young woman.

"Can I help you?"

"I'm looking for the owner of this place." Dawson held up his badge.

"That would be me. I'm Lucy Mercier."

"Is there someplace we can speak? And I need to see where your husband became ill?"

"Oh, that would be his office over there. We got it cleaned up, and I'm allowing the manager to use it right now." She smiled. "We can talk in my office."

"Get everyone out of that office, now." Dawson spoke sharper than he intended.

"Excuse me."

He strode over to the office door. "Everybody out of this office. Don't touch a thing, just get out."

"Excuse me. You can't do that," Lucy said from behind him. "Darryl, go ahead and finish this up in my office."

Dawson turned to face her, and she was furious. "What the hell do you think you're doing?"

"What do you think *you* are doing?" Dawson countered. "Crime scene, and you just let people clean up and contaminate it."

"Crime scene? They took my husband to the hospital with a stomach bug." She turned and gestured for him to follow her into another office. She shut the door behind him. "Detective, I don't know what kind of game you are playing."

"I can assure you, I don't play games, especially when it comes to murder." Dawson leaned against the door. "Want to tell me why you didn't bother to go to the hospital with your husband? Or weren't you concerned enough?"

"My husband is a big boy, Detective. He can handle a stomach bug, and we have a business to run, which happens to be in the middle of a huge sale as you can see by the amount of people here."

Dawson shook his head. "Please sit down, Mrs. Mercier."

"I don't think it's necessary. But I would like you to leave. I have things to tend to and really don't have time for this."

"Mrs. Mercier." Dawson spoke quietly, yet he couldn't hide the coldness in his tone. She looked at him and dropped into a chair.

She sighed. "What is it?"

Dawson sat down across from her. "Mrs. Mercier, your husband passed away enroute to the hospital."

She just stared at him. Slowly, she sat back in the chair and drew in a sharp breath. "Dead? That can't be."

"I'm sorry for your loss, and I'm sorry if I was a bit harsh when I—"

"You don't think it was related to those other people that died from poison?" She cut him off before he could finish his sentence.

"We don't know, but now that everything is cleaned up, we have no way of knowing until there's an autopsy."

She nodded, as tears glistened in her eyes. "Can I see him?"

"Yes, ma'am. I can drive you to the hospital if you would like. Do you have anyone you can call to be with you?"

She shook her head. "It was just the two of us... and lately we hadn't been that close. This dealership took everything we had, including any time we used to have together." She stood. "Let me just speak with the manager so he'll know I'm going to be gone. I'll lock the office so no one else can get in it."

Dawson stood and opened the door for her. He watched her hurry away to talk to the manager. He moved to the office he had just told everyone to get out of. It was empty, but the door was open. He looked in and glanced around, taking in everything. Nothing appeared to be out of place. Clean coffee cups were stacked near the Keurig. He took a last glimpse around, and he knew anything in that office that had been possibly associated with Mr. Mercier's death was gone now.

Dawson met Mrs. Mercier at the door of the dealership and drove her to the hospital. They rode in silence. He glanced over at her every so often, but she kept her face turned toward the window. She gave off no clues as to what she was thinking or feeling.

Dawson followed her into the hospital when they arrived and found Dr. Davison. Arrangements were made for Mrs. Mercier to spend some time with her husband's body while Dawson watched from outside the room. He observed that she seemed truly distraught at her husband's death. Nothing out of the ordinary.

He sighed. Dr. Davison came out of the room. "I'll contact the medical examiner's office. Mrs. Mercier has consented to an autopsy."

"Thanks," Dawson replied. "I appreciate it."

"She called a friend and said to tell you she will have a ride home."

Dawson nodded. Another body. The thought of bodies piling up before he could find the killer felt like a weight he couldn't carry. And yet, it was the same thing with every one of these cases. He was racing against the clock to find the killer before another body appeared. Dawson could only hope that Ali could get more insight with this next autopsy...something that would help him put a stop to all the madness.

thirteen

Blue fluttered in front of Cheryl's eyes as the vision started. She closed her eyes and cleared her mind. The image morphed into a scarf. Nothing else discernable. Sunlight flooded the room and Cheryl tried to focus in on something in the background to place where it was.

Nothing.

Cheryl slowly exhaled and stayed focused on the light. It started to dispel and she could see cars, not a parking lot per se, but she couldn't make out exactly what she was seeing. She sighed and opened her eyes. There had been no clear vision of a person, but she was assuming it was the car dealership she was seeing... unless there was another murder about to happen and she was seeing the next location. A blue scarf was all she really had to go on. She could imagine Wes's excitement over that bit of news.

She chuckled to herself and stood. Tea was what she needed. A cup of good, hot tea, along with a guided meditation. Maybe something else would come through.

She felt a chill as she stood in the kitchen, waiting for the kettle to boil. Something was bothering her and the chill nagged at her like a dancing child at her feet. What was she missing? It was more than Sara or Wes she was seeing. She hadn't seen anything with Ali, but there was more than murder going on. As she stared at the steam coming from the kettle, she fell into a trance-like state.

Multiple women paraded before her sight; no one she recognized. Behind the women came multiple men. Were these clients of Sara's or Sara's former boss? Cheryl had a strong sense that these murders were not centered around Sara, but were being made to shine the light on her. The question being, who was arming the spotlight?

The kettle's whistle brought her out of the trance with a start. She sighed and poured the hot water over the tea leaves in her mug. Maybe a reading of the tea leaves could give her some insight.

Ali pulled on her gloves and slid Philip Mercier out of the locker drawer to begin the autopsy. She looked over the body, inspecting all surface areas. No signs of needle marks. She started her Y cut on the torso and pulled back the chest to open the cavity after the cut was complete.

She removed the heart and examined it closely. There was no heart damage indicative of a heart attack, or even heart disease. As she opened the stomach, the velvet red coloring of the lining stood out.

Immediately, she made comments into her record, regarding signs of arsenic and possible poisoning. There was no food to indicate the man had eaten any time soon prior to his death.

Ali proceeded checking the other organs and finished up the autopsy. Her mind was already spinning on what this news would mean to Wes. This was victim number three within a matter of a week. The killer was moving fast and there would be some long nights for Wes if he was going to stop him or her before they struck again.

Death by arsenic. Ali sent the text to Wes once she got back to her office.

I was afraid of that was the reply that came in within seconds.

Ali looked at her watch. It was already five p.m. and she wasn't going to start another autopsy at this point. So, she sent another text: *I'll pick up dinner and bring it to you at the station.*

She cleaned up and decided to walk to the Greek place down the street. An order of dolmas and two grilled chicken plates was ready before she knew it, and she walked to the station, enjoying the weather. The fresh air cleared her senses. As much as she loved working in the medical examiner's office, the air was a bit stifling at times and she longed to be out in the world more than stuck in the morgue or an office without windows.

She arrived at the station and found Wes in one of the conference rooms. The victimology board was filled with pictures, markers indicating where the victims had been found, as well as comments around the board to indicate commonalities between the victims and locations.

She set the bag of food down on the table and moved to stand next to Wes. "Any new information?"

He pulled her in for a hug. "Nothing. Once again, a serial killer and I've got nothing. This one is moving fast, too."

Ali nodded. "Let's talk it through over dinner."

Wes smiled and released her. "You know me so well. I'm guessing that there isn't a bit of red meat there for me though, is there?"

"Healthy dinner." Ali smirked. "Water also."

Wes groaned. She had been pushing him to cut back on red meat, and he fought it, insisting he needed a steak once in a while. Instead, she had him eating poultry and fish. She wasn't begrudging him a steak, but all in moderation. The man would be lying on a slate after a heart attack if he didn't watch it, especially with the amount of stress his job produced. Wes fought her on eating healthy, but she knew he was a sucker for Greek food. He wouldn't complain about chicken this way.

They opened the containers and started to eat, and they were silent for a bit. Wes was facing the door, and as they were eating, Ali looked over the victimology board from her seat. Wes had already put Philip Mercier up on the board under Vic #3. The locations were nowhere near each other really and didn't seem to have a pattern. Only common thread between them was the arsenic. They knew victim one had been drinking coffee, but victim two consumed beer. No idea what victim three had been drinking. The only other common thing was each had been given a high dosage of arsenic.

"Okay." Ali sat back. "What do we know?"

"Not much at this point," Wes answered. "You've determined all three were killed with arsenic, and it was a lethal dose, not gradual." He picked up another dolma.

She nodded. "Sara had no other insight?"

"No, unfortunately. And hopefully, she's not connected in any way to this third one. Two is enough for it to look bad for her." He turned and glanced at the board. "There isn't anything that I can link between them other than Sara between the first two."

"Have you called her and asked her if she knew Mr. Mercier?" Ali asked.

"Not yet."

"You can't think about *what if she does*."

Wes smiled. "You know me that well?"

"Obviously." She winked. "There has to be something we are missing."

"Probably, but what?" He sat back and watched Ali. She met his gaze and smiled.

"If I knew that, it wouldn't be missing," Ali said. "Who else is connected to these men?" And what about jobs?"

"Vic one was a finance person, number two, coffee shop owner, and number three, car dealership owner."

"All business owners, though."

Wes sat up. "Do you think that is a common thread? How, though? Financing?"

Ali shrugged. "Maybe."

Wes pulled a file closer to him and opened it. He jotted down on a slip of paper to check into financing of all three businesses. "It might be something. Not going to hurt to check it out."

Ali agreed with it, but she was also already planning on having a talk with Sara. Maybe Wes's sister would be a little more forthcoming with her if she wasn't speaking with her brother, the cop. Try as she might, Ali knew that Sara had trouble separating her brother from his job.

fourteen

Dawson arrived at the dealership just as they were opening the next morning. He noticed that Lucy Mercier was absent from all the employees milling around. He saw the young man that had been working out of his boss's office the previous day and walked toward him.

"Detective Dawson." He held up his badge.

"Calvin Evans. What can I do for you?" He gestured to an empty office, and they both went in.

"How much interaction did you have with Philip Mercier yesterday?" Dawson sat down as Calvin took a seat across the desk from him.

"Quite a bit. I'm the finance manager here. Philip needed to approve sales that came through, but he and I would talk about finance options before the sales guy went back to the customer. We were talking almost nonstop yesterday with the sale going on. The place was packed."

"Anything out of the ordinary for that kind of day?" Dawson sat back, taking in the office. It was very similar to Mercier's office. They apparently operated on a cookie-cutter basis and there was no real personal touch to either of the offices.

"Nothing. Same type of day here at the dealership. We were busier than a normal day, but not abnormal for a big sale happening."

"Do you know what he ate or drank yesterday?"

Calvin shook his head. "Other than a cup of coffee in his hand constantly, I don't remember seeing him eat or drink anything else. That man lived on coffee."

Dawson nodded. He knew how that was. "Did you see anyone in his office?"

Calvin thought for a moment. "Other than customers we were dealing with, sales guys, and his wife, I don't recall anyone else. But I guess that doesn't really narrow it down."

Dawson sighed. That definitely did not narrow it down. "Anyone else that might know something more?"

"You can ask around the other salespeople—or the receptionist—to see if anyone asked for him directly, but it was a madhouse here yesterday. I honestly couldn't tell you the number of people I spoke with, and talked with Phil about."

"Thanks for your help." Dawson stood, shook his hand, and walked out of the office. He took in the area. The receptionist was sitting behind a desk, working on her computer.

He made his way over to her and held up his badge. "Were you working yesterday?"

"Yes, sir." She glanced up at him, breaking into a wide smile. "How can I help you?"

Her tone sounded more flirtatious than sincere.

Dawson held back an irritated sigh. "Did you have anyone ask to see Philip Mercier directly?"

She pouted her lips and gazed upward in thought. "Not really. There was one girl that came out of his office and said she was looking for him. But she left when I said he was unavailable. Said she would come back to talk to him."

"What did she look like?"

The receptionist shook her head. "I don't know. I remember she had sunglasses on and a scarf wrapped around her head, you know like she came out of a convertible. I honestly didn't pay much attention to her."

"What color scarf?" Dawson persisted.

"Blue, I think. A lightish-colored one."

Dawson handed her his business card. "If you remember anything else, please call me."

"Oh, I'm happy to call you." The receptionist winked.

He held back a snarky comment and walked away. Good lord, did he ever enjoy women like that? He couldn't remember. No one compared to Ali these days, and he never had been the sort of man to enjoy the flirtation game. He was a loner, or had been... was he still? He smiled. Didn't matter anymore. He had Ali and thanked God every day for her.

Dawson wandered into Philip's office and looked around. The door had been shut with a STAY OUT CRIME SCENE sign taped to it. He wondered if that really deterred anyone. He looked around and under the desk, being careful not to touch anything. There wasn't a thing out of place, just like he saw it the day before. Someone had cleaned up in there after Mercier was taken to the hospital and before he got there. The killer? Calvin, wanting to be in the boss's office instead of his own? Dawson imagined the killer had been long gone when Mercier actually drank the coffee with the poison in it. Coffee wasn't a stretch—considering Calvin stated that was all Mercier drank and he had a personal Keurig in his office.

Dawson left the dealership, and as he headed to his car, he took in the lot filled with vehicles. Although early, the place had quite a few people milling around. He glanced at his watch. The dealership had just opened in the time that he had been talking with Calvin and the receptionist, and if the amount of people there at opening was any indication, it would be another busy day at Mercier Motors.

fifteen

Ali had sent Sara a text late the night before, asking her to meet for coffee in the morning. She hadn't had an answer when she went to bed, but upon waking, she discovered a message from Sara giving her a location to meet at a local coffee shop at eight-thirty a.m. Ali hadn't told Wes she planned to meet Sara, not to keep it a secret, but mostly so he wouldn't want to tag along. Ali wanted this to be a girls' coffee without the investigation looming over them. Plus, she was dying to get to know Sara better.

Wes seemed to have had a load lifted once he and Sara started to talk again. They still had a long way to go, but they seemed to be on a good road to recovery.

Ali arrived at the coffeeshop before Sara and ordered a Mocha Latte. She found a quiet spot in the corner where they wouldn't be interrupted. Within five minutes, Sara came in. Ali waved and nodded when Sara gestured to the ordering line.

Once Sara settled into the chair across from Ali, they both took a sip of their drinks. Ali felt more relaxed, and Sara looked as if she did, too. "I was so glad to get your text this morning agreeing to meet me," Ali stated.

"Are you kidding?" Sara smiled. "I was thrilled to hear from you. I need all the dirt on my brother I can get."

Ali had longed for a sister growing up, and this exchange in itself brought her a sense of that desire finally coming to fruition. "I thought it might be good for us to get to know each other a bit better. I've heard so much from Wes about you, from your childhood, that it will be nice to get to know the adult you."

Sara chuckled. "Wes's memories might not be all that accurate. Did he tell you how much of a pest he was in those days?" Ali watched Sara smile again as she seemed to drift away into a memory.

"You've missed him over the years." It was a statement, not a question. Ali could see it written all over Sara's face.

Sara nodded. "I have. More than he will ever know. And there is a part of me that is so sorry that I didn't allow him to connect with me sooner. I knew he would be unhappy with my life choices, but deep down I also knew he was my brother and despite being disappointed in me, he would always be there. I let my fear get in the way of that."

"Well, the important thing is now you two have reconnected. Maybe not under the best of circumstances, but whatever the reason that brought you two together, the past shouldn't matter."

Sara took a sip of her coffee. "You know, it shouldn't matter. But I keep putting myself in his shoes. He was so angry that day when he came face to face with me in the interrogation room...I can't say I blame him. I probably would have been furious, too."

"Was it really just your job that kept you away from him?" Ali asked.

"No, I suppose not. I knew I was in a profession that Wes would have a problem with...not so much Wes, my brother, but the law-upholding part of him. I guess I didn't think about the hurt he was feeling."

Ali nodded. "You realize all those nights he spent searching for you...he never would give up."

Sara kept her eyes on her cup. "I know." Her voice came out in a whisper, and Ali could see the tears shimmering on her eyelashes. Ali reached a hand over and covered Sara's, knowing a change of topic was necessary.

"There was another murder, Sara." Ali made a point to keep her tone low.

"Oh, no. Please, not someone I know."

Ali shrugged. "Are you acquainted with anyone at Mercier Motors?"

Sara shook her head. "No, not personally. I can see if they were a part of the former records I have."

Ali nodded. "I was hoping that was the case. We just can't seem to find any other connections between the victims."

"Is Wes thinking I have something to do with this?" Sara's voice sounded strained, and Ali knew this had been weighing heavily on her.

"No, he doesn't," Ali said. "But he is worried about you. Is there anyone you can think of who would want to make it seem like you are involved?"

Sara sat without moving for a moment, but Ali could tell her thoughts were spinning. "Not that I can think of," she finally said. "I have a very small circle of friends, and I don't believe I have any enemies. Really, the only girlfriend I have is my best friend, Evie."

"No issues between the two of you?"

Sara adamantly shook her head. "No way. She's had her own set of issues and we rely heavily on each other for comfort, support. She's struggled a lot growing up, and I think now she still struggles, but doesn't let on to half of what she actually goes through."

"Any clients that you have recently broken ties with?" Ali frowned.

"No. I also keep my clients to a handful. I prefer quality over quantity." Sara searched Ali's face. "Do you really think someone is trying to set me up?"

"I have no idea. I'm just trying to look at all angles." Ali shrugged. "Wes is working hard to try to get ahead of this killer."

"My brother never liked to lose, and I imagine having multiple bodies piling up is putting him on edge."

Ali decided to switch gears, and they talked about getting together and having a shopping day...a true girls' day out. Ali glanced at her watch. "Unfortunately, I have to get to work."

☠   ☠   ☠

Sara chilled a bottle of white wine. She pulled out appetizers and started heating them up. Mozzarella sticks and marinara. Evie's favorite. With all that had been going on with Wes, Sara felt that she had been distant to Evie and decided to have a girls' night. Appetizers, wine, and a good chat fest. She had just set the timer for the oven when the doorbell rang.

She pulled open the door and Evie stood there with a bottle of wine and a bag of popcorn. "Let the girls' night begin."

"I've got mozzarella sticks in the oven and a bottle in the fridge. Do we need to chill that one?" Sara moved toward the kitchen as she spoke.

"Might as well get this one cold, too. I have a feeling it will be a two-bottle night." Evie followed Sara and put it in the fridge. "So, what's on the agenda other than eating and drinking?"

"Well, we can just sit and talk. I feel like we haven't had a chance to really talk lately...or we can watch a movie." Sara closely studied her friend. "Your choice."

Evie winked. "We always have so much to talk about. And you're right, we haven't really had the chance lately. So much we need to catch up on. I'm dying to know what happened on your blind date."

"Not much to tell about the date, really. He was a jerk, and I left early. However, apparently, he was killed that night, and I was the last to see him before he died."

"Girl, what are you doing killing off men? Sam, and now this guy?" Evie joked.

"Not even a joking matter, Eve. It doesn't look good, and I've been questioned a couple of times now by the police." Sara pulled the pan of cheese sticks from the oven.

"Are you kidding?" Evie poured the wine. "They don't really think you had anything to do with it, do they?"

"No, I guess not. But it is a bit disconcerting when not only one, but now *two* men have died either in my presence or right after I left them."

"I can imagine. What are you going to do?" Evie carried the glasses to the living room.

Sara followed her with the appetizers. "I have no idea. I'm almost scared to meet any of my clients or go on another date."

"You can't shy away from your job, or not have a personal life, just because of this."

Sara shrugged. "No, but I don't want to take any chances. If someone is targeting people I know—"

"Not people you know," Evie interrupted. "That other one was a blind date. You didn't know him, did you?"

"No, I didn't. Although he said I had been recommended to him by a *friend*. I don't know who, and he hinted at knowing what my job was. I don't get it. I met him on the dating app."

"Sometimes people go on those apps to meet people that they already have their eye on. Who knows? Maybe it was someone watching you for a while?"

Sara stared at her friend. "Why would someone want to manipulate a meeting through a dating site? If he knew the business I was in, why not just approach me if that was what he wanted? I don't know...it was just strange the way the whole thing went down."

They enjoyed their snacks in silence, only making an occasional comment or joke. Once the mozzarella sticks were gone, they both leaned back on their respective ends of the couch and sighed.

"It's been way too long since we've done this," Evie said. "I've missed it."

"I know. We definitely need to do it more often." Sara stood and went to grab the bottle of wine to refill their glasses. When she came back to the living room, Evie had put on the radio and was singing along to Carly Simon's *You're So Vain*.

"Anyone in particular you're singing that song about?" Sara asked.

Evie just smiled and sang louder. Sara joined in and refilled their glasses. As the song ended, Sara turned the music down so they could talk. "What's been happening with *you?*" Sara asked.

"Nothing."

"What happened to that guy you were seeing?"

Evie smiled, but it looked forced. "He decided he wanted to see other people." She shrugged.

poison

Sara watched her, trying to see deeper into her demeanor. "Just like that. No other explanation?"

"None."

"Well, that sucks," Sara said. "I'm sorry, Evie."

"No big deal. I'm just not that lucky in the love department, I guess."

Sara raised her glass. "You and me both, girl."

sixteen

Ali curled up on the couch with her laptop. Wes had stayed late again at the station to try to go through some more notes to gain insight into any more connections. Ali opened the laptop and started her search of female serial killers who had killed with arsenic. As per previous cases Wes had solved, there had been a killer murdering their victims in the same fashion as a serial killer from in the past. One that had already passed on, and whether or not it was reincarnation, it was something eerily similar—though Ali leaned more toward believing in reincarnation. But did that mean these killers were born this way, and if so, what triggered them to start killing?

Many people were ill at ease with the thought of someone reincarnating, yet Ali felt in some respects, it brought peace to people. They could think they might come back again someday and maybe do things better than they had that time around, or maybe be reunited with a loved one. For whatever reason, Ali liked the thought of it. Now, did she feel at peace thinking that a serial killer was back again to wreak more havoc in the world? Not in the least. But in the same vein as the past two killers who Wes had caught, it was worth looking into.

Ali pulled up Google and immediately typed in serial killers who used arsenic. The list that populated was more than she had imagined. The top names were Mary Ann Cotton, Amy Archer-Gilligan, and Nannie Doss. Mary Ann Cotton had killed ten children, and Ali pushed that name to the side. Certainly, there hadn't been any children involved. Amy Archer-Gilligan had worked in a nursing home and killed off elderly people. Again, not following the pattern that had been established so far.

The third name was *The Giggling Granny*, Nannie Doss. The woman had been a deluded romantic—marrying multiple times and killing her husbands. Her fourth husband had miraculously survived. It just was not a fatal dose that was given. Though Nannie Doss had poisoned her husbands, she had also killed her mother, sister, grandson, and mother-in-law over time. So far, in the current case, the only people who had been killed were men. Could Nannie Doss be a possibility?

The clearing of a throat startled Ali from her research, and she snapped her head up to see Wes grinning at her. She hadn't even heard the door open.

He chuckled. "I had hoped to warn you I was here so you wouldn't be scared."

"I wasn't scared." She stuck out her tongue at him.

"Whatcha doing?" Wes sat down next to her on the couch and pulled her legs over his.

"Research." Ali grinned.

"Do I dare ask what?"

She shrugged. "Whether you dare or not, I'm going to tell you. I got thinking about our other cases–Lizzie Borden and Lavinia Fisher." She paused and watched as Wes slowly shook his head. "Oh, yeah, there are multiple women that killed using arsenic."

"You're going the route of someone reincarnated again? Or do you just think it is a possession?" Wes asked.

"I'm thinking reincarnation. A possession would be a different type of killing I would imagine."

"I don't know, Ali. This seems so farfetched."

"Does it, though? Was it farfetched that Beth was killing with an axe just like Lizzie did, and then asked you to call her Lizzie? Or when Olivia killed like Lavinia Fisher, and then said the same final words Lavinia did before she killed herself?" Ali took a breath. "It seems like a reasonable theory to me."

"I know you think it is, and on some level, I agree with you, but on the other hand...it feels like grasping at straws. And even if it is, that brings us no closer to knowing who the actual killer is."

Ali nodded. "I know. I didn't say it was a perfect theory."

Wes sighed, leaned his head back, and closed his eyes. "I don't know why I have to handle these wackos. It would be nice to just deal with a normal killer and not these ghosts from the past."

"Why do you think you keep getting them? Why is it that this area seems to be inundated with them lately?" Ali circled her fingers on Wes's temple.

He smiled. "Feels good. And I don't know if three is inundated, but it's definitely three too many." He opened his eyes, turned his head, and looked at her.

"I just keep thinking there has to be a reason. Have you discussed with Cheryl what she knows about rein-carnation and my theory?"

Wes lifted an eyebrow. "No. Is that something I should have thought about doing?"

Ali rolled her eyes. "Apparently not. I will continue to walk you through everything, and you take all the glory when the crime is solved."

Wes laughed. "What exactly is it you think Cheryl can tell us? That she has had one of her woo-woo visions and she suddenly knows the reason we're getting all these killers?"

Ali widened her eyes. "Woo-woo visions?" She shook her head. "Granted it sounds farfetched when you say it like that, but you have to admit, Cheryl knows things that no one else would. And regardless of whether you believe it or not, I wonder if there is a possibility that these women have been called to this area."

Wes stared at her. She could see it all over his face that he was trying hard not to make some snide comment. "I don't even know what to say to that. You think they have been *called* to this area? How does that even work?"

She shrugged. "I have no idea, which is why I said, ask Cheryl."

Wes slowly smiled at her. "Or... *you* could ask her. Then you would know the right questions to ask and I wouldn't have to deal with it at all. You can fill me in later."

Ali harumphed, which made his smile widen even further. "Fine," she relented. "I'll call Cheryl tomorrow and have this conversation with her, and then... maybe I will share it with you."

"See, I knew I kept you around for a reason." Wes pulled her close and tenderly kissed her, teasing her until she sighed softly and leaned against him.

He grabbed the laptop, put it on the couch, then gathered Ali into his arms and started for the bedroom. "Let's go to bed." She snuggled against him and nibbled on his neck.

seventeen

Dawson studied the victimology board. Still no links between the victims. He had pulled financials on all three of the businesses that had been owned by the victims, yet there was no link between those either. Victim number one's spouse came right out and said Sara had killed him because they were going to break up. Sara had no indication that Sam was going to break things off with her, so Dawson couldn't put much stock in that. Sara, he would imagine, would know if Sam was going to walk away from the business arrangement.

Victim number two's fiancée had thought he was faithful to her, and it had been a shock to know that he had been out meeting other women. Dawson couldn't put her in the category of suspect if she was unaware of what had been going on.

E.L. Reed

Which led him to victim number three. He hadn't dug up anything on the man to indicate he had been unfaithful to his wife. Dawson couldn't help but wonder if Sara—or at least her former boss—was somehow related to all of the murders. Sara had known the first two victims but denied knowing the third. That didn't mean that she didn't know him in passing, though, or that he hadn't been involved in the prostitution business when the former owner ran it.

Frustration coursed through him as he took a sip of coffee. He pulled out his cellphone and dialed Cheryl Porter's number. Maybe Ali was right, and he needed a different perspective.

"Good morning, Wes," Cheryl answered the phone.

"Good thing for caller ID," Dawson quipped.

"You think I wouldn't know it was you even without it?"

He laughed. He may not believe in what she did, but he certainly enjoyed her sense of humor. "Can we meet and talk? I...well Ali has a theory she thought I should run by you and get your thoughts on."

"I thought you preferred Ali to talk to me directly."

"Why would you say that?" Dawson asked.

Soft laughter came through the phone. "Ali and I are meeting in thirty minutes at Brew House, which I think is your favorite place. Care to join us?"

"Sounds good." They both hung up without a *goodbye* and Dawson reached for his keys. He wanted to get there early, and hopefully, Deb would have picked up her fiancé's phone and would have some insight for him.

Dawson walked into the coffee shop and ordered a coffee. He spotted Deb near the back, and her eyes met his. She waved but was busy talking with some staff members, so Dawson continued to a table off to the side. He sat back and watched the people come in and out. There were a few patrons sitting at tables, many on computers or phones. However, most of the customers were taking their beverages and/or food to go.

"Detective Dawson," Deb said as she approached the table. "So nice to see you again."

He stood. "Nice to see *you* again."

"I'm glad you're here. I picked up Daniel's belongings yesterday and his phone was dead. After charging it all night, I finally managed to get into it this morning."

"Anything unusual that you came across?" Dawson asked.

"The dating site as you said was on there, and he had a few text messages that I was surprised by."

Dawson gestured for her to sit and waited for her to continue.

"There were a bunch of text messages from someone that he didn't have named in his phone. Just listed under *her*. Obviously, he had been seeing her regularly for a while. However, the last text was telling her he didn't want to see her anymore. No explanation. That was it, and she hadn't replied. I don't know if that was the end of it, or if he saw her again."

"When was that text...where he broke up with her?" Dawson asked.

"About a week before he died. But the activity on the dating site was right up until the night of his death. He apparently was talking with a few different women and had arranged to meet two of them that night at different times." Deb shrugged. "I guess I didn't know him at all."

"I'm sorry, Deb, that you found out this way," Dawson said, studying her. She was a strong woman. He had yet to see her shed tears, although she had been obviously upset, and she had continued to step up and run the business. She was concerned with her employees and Dawson just knew she would come out on the other side of this stronger than ever. "Do you think I could get copies of those messages?"

Deb nodded. "I already thought of that and printed out all the messages on the dating site for you, and I downloaded all the text messages from this *her* and printed them out. They're in the office. I'll bring them out. I hate to run, and I'll get them out to you before you leave, but I need to meet with one of our vendors right now."

"No problem. I'm meeting someone here, and I'll check with the register before I leave if you haven't brought them out." Dawson smiled. "Thank you."

"Anything to help solve this." Deb returned his smile before leaving the table.

He didn't have to wait long before he saw Cheryl walk in with Ali, chatting away beside her. He waved to them and both ladies settled into the chairs—Ali to his right, and Cheryl across the table from him.

"I was surprised to hear from you," Cheryl said with a grin, "though not surprised at all to hear from Ali."

"Yes, you know Ali is much more receptive to this nonsense than I am."

Cheryl snorted. "Nonsense...I'm so glad you called, Ali. At least you are reasonable."

Dawson got comfortable and looked to Ali to let her lead the conversation.

Ali sat forward in her chair. "Reincarnation. The last three cases have been killers killing with the same MO as a past serial killer. Is it possible that these people have been reincarnated?"

Cheryl glanced at Dawson, and then turned her attention back to Ali. "That's an interesting theory. So, who is this latest killer supposedly?"

Ali pulled the notes she had made the previous night from her purse. "Nannie Doss. Although there have been multiple serial killers over the years that have killed with arsenic, she seemed to be the closest fit."

"Yes, arsenic would definitely be a female's choice for poisoning, but it undeniably isn't as easy to get as it was years ago when you could go to the pharmacy and say you had a rat problem. Back then, they would just hand you arsenic to take care of the rodents."

"But it's not impossible to get," Dawson said. "Especially on the internet these days." He shook his head. "Damn if you can't get just about anything online nowadays."

"True." Cheryl tipped her head to the side. "It's an interesting concept. So how can I help with this?"

Dawson shrugged. "You know I don't know much about this reincarnation stuff. I guess I need to know how all this works if someone believed in it. Not sure even if I know how it would work, if that would bring us any closer to finding the killer."

"It probably wouldn't," Cheryl replied. "Even if they are reincarnated, it wouldn't tell us who they became in this life."

"That's what I figured. But fill me in anyway."

"Well, reincarnation is simply the rebirth of someone. If someone dies, they would be reborn into a different person."

"Okay, wait. So, say with my first case of the Lizzie Borden wannabe, you're saying if they are reincarnated, then they are born that way. This wouldn't be just all of a sudden, this person is there in them?" Dawson scowled.

"Right. Lizzie Borden would have come back as that killer when the girl was born."

"That doesn't make sense to me," Dawson said.

Cheryl laughed. "That's not to say that this girl— if Lizzie had been reincarnated—that she would have automatically started killing. There would have been a trauma that would have triggered those memories and actions."

Wes nodded. "Okay. In that particular case, we know there was a trauma. But if it is more sudden, wouldn't it be more of a *possession* of this killer's spirit in someone's body?"

"Could be. Do you believe in spirits possessing people quicker than reincarnation?" Cheryl grinned at him. "But you are right that it doesn't give you any insight as to who it is, but it might give you the why they are doing what they are doing."

Ali had been quiet, letting Dawson put his thoughts out there, but she laid a hand on his arm and looked eager to speak. He gave a nod. Hell, he was relieved she wanted to say something. "The real question is," she said and turned to Cheryl, "could there be a reason for three killers to be reincarnated and called to a certain area?"

"That's an interesting thought. Occasionally, spirits can be called to a certain area. Then it becomes more of, is it a reincarnation or a spirit coming through and attaching themselves to a person...yes, more of a possession. I'm not sure I'm inclined to think that way, but I guess it could be possible."

Ali sighed. "It was a thought. I don't know, but I do know there is too much coincidence with past female killers for these murderers to just start randomly killing in this area."

Dawson leaned over and kissed Ali's cheek. "I'll let you two hash it out. I've got to get back to the station and look for some real leads."

He got up from the table, and as he turned toward the register, Deb laid a large envelopment on the counter and pointed at it for him. He nodded, grabbed it, and left to dive into another aspect of the murders.

eighteen

Dinners between Ali and Wes had become almost nonexistent since the murders unfolded. He spent all his time working on the case, and if she wasn't at the morgue, she was home eating alone, waiting for him to get there. She had taken to staying at his place so they could at least see each other for a few minutes when he got home to sleep for a couple of hours.

She had been perusing the cupboards looking for something simple to make for dinner when the doorbell rang. She opened the door to see Sara standing there holding a bag. "Dinner?"

Ali stepped back. "Come on in. I was just looking to see what I could make."

"Well, it's not much. Chicken wings and salad." Sara stepped in. "I figured Wes wouldn't be here, and I could use some company."

"I welcome the company, and you're right, Wes is

still working. Long hours when he's in the middle of an investigation."

Sara pulled out the dinner while Ali grabbed paper plates, napkins, and silverware. She then reached into the fridge and grabbed the carafe of water.

"Water okay, or would you prefer something else?" Ali asked.

"Water's good."

They filled their plates and started eating. The silence was comfortable. After the initial hunger died down, Ali sat back. "What's on your mind, Sara?"

Sara smiled. "Why do you think something's on my mind? Can't I just want to have dinner with a friend?"

Ali raised an eyebrow. "You could, but I'm guessing there is more to it than that."

Sara sighed. "I don't know. Lately, I just feel kind of lonely, I guess. Now that Sam is gone, it seems like business has slowed down. And Evie, well she seems to be busy and we haven't had time to really sit and chat."

"I understand that Sam's death could hurt the business, but do your other clients really know that he was a client and what happened? Would it have that kind of effect?"

"Hmm..." Sara sat in thought for a moment. "Maybe not. I guess I'm feeling like I don't want to go out with any of the clients right now, though nothing was really lined up. I guess I'm missing Evie more than I realized, though it's not unusual for us to have spurts like this where we don't talk much. We both lead busy lives."

Ali nodded. "What does Evie do?"

"She does consultant work. Though being honest, I'm not sure on what. We got to know each other back when I was with Rick and she was on the streets. We friended each other when I left Rick and bonded over the fact that we were trying to get off the streets. Things weren't that great for either of us. I kind of glossed over the extent of things when I was talking about it with Wes. I don't want him upset about the way things were. I chose my life, and I have dealt with the consequences of my decisions. I just don't want to have to rehash it with my brother."

Ali picked at her food, as Sara continued. "She had a tough life and we just kind of bonded over our own sob stories. Don't get me wrong, my life wasn't near as bad as most girls that end up on the streets. I came from a decent home, albeit my parents were strict and never let us do anything. I was more of a rebel than my sisters and wanted out."

"So why didn't you just go home after things didn't work out with Rick?" Ali asked.

"I felt like my parents would have been unforgiving, and I didn't want Wes to know what a failure I had been."

Ali watched Sara. "You don't really believe Wes would have considered you a failure, do you?"

Sara shrugged. "Maybe not, but we had been really close, and he was upset when I left."

"That's understandable, considering how close you were." Ali pushed her plate aside. "What does Evie have to say about your business and what happened with Sam? I'm assuming she knows about the business."

"She does to a point. She doesn't know that I took Madame's records to continue with my own stuff. She thinks some men that I had worked with before just found me. She was never involved in that business with Madame, and I never went into a lot of detail of what I did. I'm sure she knew there was sex involved, and she knew Sam was a regular and favorite of mine."

"Would she have any reason to be jealous of you?" Ali asked.

"I doubt it. She is the first one there when I need something, or when *she* needs something. We're more like sisters than friends."

nineteen

Things hadn't gone as planned so far, but I was determined to make this work. I was so tired of playing second fiddle to everyone else around me. Men used me, and then threw me away for someone younger, prettier, or just *the marrying type*, which apparently, I was not—according to those men.

I could slowly pick them off one by one, but it wasn't getting me anywhere. There had to be a focus of getting the men to really come around and realize what they were going to miss. I hated being forced to take their lives into my own hands. I didn't want to be that woman. I wanted their love and commitment, not to be a side piece or just second best if their first choice wasn't available.

I pulled the box toward me that had the weddings rings in it. I wanted more than the life I was leading. Who would be my next target? It was a rhetorical thought as I knew exactly who my next victim would be. I wanted to live a quiet life, a happy life, but so far that had been a far-reaching thought and dream for me.

I plucked the next vial from the basket on the counter. There were only three left. I knew exactly who two of them were for and a thought started weaving through my mind for the third. I smiled in a sinister way, lifting the corner of my lips. Yes, it would be perfect...the icing on the cake.

Michael had pursued me—and don't get me wrong—he had his major pros, most importantly, being that he was a stockbroker and was loaded. However, I didn't seem to be the first choice for him. I had heard rumors that he had been pursuing the competition until he was rejected, and then all of a sudden, I looked good. I researched him thoroughly, and not only was I second choice for mistress, but he was also married. Not the right man for those golden rings I had hidden away. Nevertheless, we had a date tonight.

I took my time dressing. The slinky black dress clung to my curves, and with my high-heeled black pumps, my legs went on forever. I winked at myself in the mirror before applying my makeup. My new wig was the same color and style as Sara's. If he wanted her, he would get her. This would be a very telling night.

I showed up at the restaurant and his eyes widened when he saw me come through the door. I slowed my walk toward him, allowing his eyes to roam over me, taking in every bit of the transformation. He smiled as I approached him. Oh, this was going to be fun. In the back of my mind, a memory emerged of a man telling me what a slut I looked like and how this would be the downfall of the family. I cringed inwardly, wondering where that thought came from. I vaguely recognized the voice, yet couldn't place it.

"Shall we?" Michael had made reservations, and the table was ready. He walked behind me with his hand on the small of my back as I followed the hostess, who had been standing by, waiting for me. This restaurant was not my usual scene, so much posher than I would normally visit. But if all went well, my life would be taking a turn, and soon, money would not be an object for me. Hell, if Sara could do this, I could do it better. That girl, Layla, as she called herself, had her choice of men. I had been watching her for years since Madame had died. There was something Sara was hiding.

"You look stunning," Michael whispered in my ear as he pulled the chair out for me.

"Thank you. You don't look so bad yourself." Time to pour on the sweetness. I put my purse in my lap, comforted by the vial inside that would either be used tonight, or *not* if things went well. It was a safety net, though. I refused to get caught up in a triangle, and this man needed to prove he was worthy of me.

We ordered drinks and our meals. Once the drinks came, I relaxed a bit after the first couple of sips. I shouldn't be nervous about tonight, but there was a lot riding on Michael coming aboard. He was a stockbroker and had quite an impressive portfolio. The man would be set for life, and if he already had a mistress, he wasn't too concerned with his vows to his wife. The question became, could I get him to cut the mistress loose? I would love for him to cut the wife loose, too, and then I could wiggle my way in and take the money. I would be set for life. I did have a handful of rights.

A memory flashed again of a wedding at a courthouse. *Number four and none the wiser* was the thought that ran through my mind a few times. Who the hell's memory was this? I startled and tried to refocus on what Michael was saying to me.

"Are you okay?" His voice broke through my thoughts.

I nodded. "Have had a bit of a headache earlier. It's almost gone—just given a twinge every so often. I think it's the lightening," I lied.

He nodded. He didn't really seem to care if I was in distress. He was probably thinking about what he was going to get from me after dinner. My dress was certainly telling him he'd get lucky.

The meal came, and we ate in comfortable silence. I pushed my plate aside and sat back. "So, Michael, what exactly do you want?"

He grinned. "You know what I want."

I winked. "Beyond that. Don't be coy."

He sat back and sighed. "One of those business-type people. Okay, I can see this will not be a *just go with the flow* type deals." He watched me for a few seconds. "You've changed your hair. You know, it looks just like Sara's."

I nodded and waited.

"Is that because you know I wanted to be a client of hers?"

I nodded again. "Isn't this the look you were after?" I kept my voice low.

He leaned forward. "What game are you playing?"

I followed his lead and leaned in just enough that he could glimpse down my dress. "Not a game, Michael. You know Sara and I are in the same business. I can give you what she refuses to, and let's be honest, I can guarantee you will be much happier with me."

He chuckled. "You can guarantee it?"

"Absolutely. You are sitting here with me and not her, aren't you? She didn't think you were good enough for her."

I had found the mark and his smile twisted into a frown. His eyes narrowed as he looked at me. "Don't bait me."

"I don't consider telling the truth baiting you, dear. The fact of the matter is you need to make a decision. There is an offer on the table for us to work together, you can accept it or not."

He watched me, amusement playing across his face. "So, this is a *take it or leave it* moment." He snapped his mouth shut as the waitress approached.

"Can I get you anything else?" she asked.

"I'll have another beer, please," he said and turned to me.

"Another martini, please."

The waitress nodded and strolled off.

"I say we enjoy our drinks, and then go our separate ways." He watched me carefully as he made his bold proclamation, and I kept my face neutral. "I'm not sure *this* is really what interests me." He glanced up and down at me.

I nodded. "A final drink then, before we go our separate ways."

"Excuse me. I see a colleague I must say hello to." He stood and walked off as the waitress returned with the drinks.

"Thank you," I sweetly said.

The waitress moved away, and I pulled Michael's beer close to me with one hand and reached for the vial with the other. I glimpsed around. No one was paying any attention, so I dumped the vial contents into the beer and pushed it back to its place in front of Michael's plate.

I sipped my drink, and when Michael finally came back to the table I was about done. It was obvious as soon as he made his decision, I was just an inconvenience to him now. "Well, Michael, I think I'll call it a night." I smiled. "It was a pleasure, and I certainly wish you the best of luck."

He stood as I rose and had sat back down swigging his beer before I completely left the building. I stood outside in the shadows watching him laugh and talk with some other men that stopped by his table. I checked my watch, and after fifteen minutes when Michael stood to leave, I turned and walked away.

twenty

The phone ringing pulled Dawson from his sleep. He looked at the clock. Four a.m. With a groan, he picked up the phone and answered it.

"Sir, Brown here. There is another body."

"Text me the location. I'm on my way." Dawson hung up. He glanced over at Ali lying next to him. He had hoped the phone hadn't woken her, too, but he discovered she was awake and watching him.

"I'm up. I'm coming with you." She got out of bed and headed to the bathroom.

"You don't need to," Dawson called to her, knowing full well that she wouldn't listen.

She stuck her head out of the bathroom and smiled at him. "Why do you even bother?"

He shrugged. "I'm leaving in ten. Be ready, or I leave without you."

She laughed. "We both know I'll be making coffee, and you won't be going anywhere without the coffee."

He grimaced. She was right. He pulled on jeans and shirt. "I'll make the coffee."

They were out the door in ten minutes, both with a travel mug of coffee in hand. Whether Dawson wanted to admit it or not, it was moments like this that he cherished. He never thought he would have this sort of relationship with his type of job. Someone next to him, ready to jump up and accompany him to a crime scene. Granted, her office would be called anyway, but it was still nice to know that their lives were so intertwined in a good way.

They arrived at the scene and both ducked under crime tape. It was still early enough that there weren't a lot of people milling about hoping to catch a glimpse of whatever horror awaited them. The scene corded off was at the end of an alley. Dawson shivered as he remembered the dead bodies in the alleys of the hatchet murders. He prayed this was not *another* serial killer, and not that he wanted it related to his case, but it had to be if they called him. He saw Brown talking with a young woman. She had red eyes, evidence of tears she had recently spilt.

"What do we have, Brown?" Dawson said as he came up behind them.

Officer Brown turned to him. "Sir, this is Amelia Smythe. She was on her way to work this morning and came across the body."

"You get an early start to the day, Miss Smythe." Dawson smiled at her.

"Please, call me Amelia. I work at the bakery around the corner. I start usually about three-thirty every morning to get the bread started. I cut through this alley to our back door."

Dawson nodded. "So, you cut through here at three-thirty, and what did you find?"

She pointed at a body that Ali was now bent over, examining. "I didn't realize he was dead at first. I figured it was a drunk that had passed out. I started to just go by him, but then I noticed the vomit all over the place and thought I should check him."

Dawson nodded. "And this was at three-thirty?"

Amelia confirmed. "I called 9-1-1, and then called my boss to let him know I was going to be late. I stayed here like they told me to so you could talk to me, but I have to say I really need to get to work."

"I understand," Dawson said. "Go ahead. If it's okay, I'll stop by your work and talk with you a little later. What would be a good time for you?"

"If you could make it after nine, sir, I'll be able to take a break then."

Dawson nodded. "I'll see you then. Go ahead, but please keep things under wraps until you and I can talk."

"I will." She scurried off.

Dawson made his way over to Ali. "What do you think?"

"From the amount of vomit and the dried foam around his lips, my guess is that he was poisoned. But we will have to wait for the autopsy for definite answers. I can say time of death was probably between ten and midnight."

Dawson frowned. Brown stood next to him. "His license says he is Michael Sydney," Brown said before Dawson could even ask. Brown handed him a piece of paper that had the man's address on it.

"Thanks." Dawson turned toward him. "I really would love it if you would come to the State Police and work with me full time." Dawson had mentioned this a couple of times to Brown, and Brown seemed excited by the prospect, but then a murder would come up and time was limited.

"I definitely am thinking of it, sir...Dawson," Brown corrected.

Dawson grinned. "I'll break you yet of that *sir* crap."

twenty-one

Dawson pulled up in front of the house at 23 Martin Way. One thing for sure was that most of the victims in this case had money. He stared at the large, sprawling building. Too flashy for Dawson's taste, as it oozed new money. He exited the vehicle and started to the front door. The upcoming conversation was the kind that wasn't easy—the sort he would never get used to.

He rang the doorbell and waited. It was only five a.m. and he hated to ring someone so early. A woman who looked like she was ready to leave for some type of event opened the door. She was dressed in a skirt and sweater with heels, makeup perfect. *Who the hell rolls out of bed that way?*

"Mrs. Sydney?" Dawson asked.

"Yes. What can I do for you?" she responded.

"Ma'am, I'm Detective Dawson with the Connecticut State Police." He flashed his credentials. "May I come in?"

"If you're looking for my good-for-nothing husband, I assume he is either at his office or at his whore's place."

Dawson kept his expression neutral. "I'm here to speak to you, ma'am."

She stepped back from the door and gestured him to enter. "Please, call me Brianna."

Dawson closed the door behind him and followed her into a living room where they both sat down. "Ma'am, when was the last time you saw your husband?"

"Last night. He was going out. Said he had a business meeting at the Padmore Steakhouse. That typically is code for *he has a date*." She crossed her legs. "I don't bother to ask anymore."

Dawson watched her carefully. She didn't appear angry at the man. "Ma'am, we found your husband this morning. We don't know the extent of what happened, but Michael was found dead just a block down the street from the restaurant."

"Dead?" Mrs. Sydney sat up straighter—something he didn't think possible. "I don't understand."

"We're waiting on the autopsy, but we will need you to come to the morgue to identify him." She nodded. "Brianna, do you have someone you can call to come be with you?"

She looked at him in confusion for a moment. "Oh, yes. I'll call my sister. She will come over and stay with me. Do you think someone did this to him, or was he robbed?"

"We don't know yet. I'll keep you updated once we start getting more information."

She nodded. "Do you mind if I call my sister, and then we can meet you at the morgue?"

Dawson stood. "Of course." He handed her his

card. "Just give me a call, and I'll meet you there when you're ready." Dawson started to leave, and then turned back. "Do you happen to have a recent photo of your husband?"

She pulled out her phone and opened her photos. She airdropped it to Dawson's phone. "Here you go."

"Thanks." He let himself out as Brianna Sydney frantically tapped on the screen of her cellphone.

He sat in his car a moment, thinking back over the conversation he had just had with Brianna. She seemed to show genuine shock, yet not real grief. Not uncommon for some grief to be displayed later after the initial shock wore off, but he had a familiar sense that more than one wife of the victims were not really that upset.

He turned and headed toward the Padmore Steakhouse. With any luck, he would get some information there about the previous night and his victim. He needed a break. He looked at his watch, still too early for a good steak. He smiled as he thought of taking Ali there for a night out once this case was over and done with.

He arrived at the restaurant and found a man inside behind the bar taking inventory. "Can I help you, sir?"

Dawson held out his credentials. "Detective Dawson. I'm here regarding a gentleman that was here last night for dinner."

"I might need a little more to go on than that." The man smiled and held out his hand. "I'm the owner, Jack Livingston."

Dawson shook his hand, and then pulled out his phone. He opened up the picture the victim's wife had sent him. "Do you know this man?"

Jack took the phone and looked at it closely. "I don't know him personally, but he's in here quite regularly. Usually with other men, I would assume business clients or colleagues. Last night he was with a female."

Dawson took his phone back. "Do you know who waited on him and the girl?"

"Eleanor did. She should be in soon. She worked last night but has the day shift today." He looked at his watch and nodded. "She's typically early, so I would expect her any minute. Can I get you anything while you wait? Coffee?"

Dawson nodded. "Coffee would be great." He slid onto the bar stool and doctored up the coffee Jack placed in front of him.

"I've got to finish my inventory before we open, if you don't mind."

"You go ahead. I'm just going to enjoy the quiet for a few minutes with my coffee."

The man nodded and continued on with his business. Dawson had just finished his coffee when a young woman came through the doors. "I'm here, Jack."

"Eleanor. This is Detective Dawson. He needs to speak to you about one of our customers last night. I think he was at your table."

The girl smiled at Dawson. "What can I help you with?"

Dawson pulled out the phone and showed her the picture. "Yes, he sat at my table last night. He was a beer guy, and the girl he was with drank martinis." She handed the phone back. "I tend to remember their drinks as opposed to anyone's names."

"That's okay. What can you tell me about the two of them? Where they getting along, fighting?" Dawson asked.

"They seemed to be getting along, but then they ordered a second drink, and he left the table to talk to people. She sat there alone drinking her drink. When he came back to the table, she left and he stayed for probably another half hour."

Dawson nodded. "Did she look angry when she left?"

Eleanor shook her head. "I wouldn't say *angry*. She didn't look happy, but more indifferent."

"Can you describe her?"

She closed her eyes as if trying to picture her in her mind, her fingers moving beside her. Then her eyes re-opened, and she took a breath. "She was dressed up in a sexy black dress...you know one of those that clings in all the right places. Dark hair, shoulder length. I'd say she wasn't really tall, though hard to tell since she was wearing heels. I don't think I can give you much more than that. I was pretty busy last night."

Dawson nodded. He picked up his phone and ri-fled through his pictures. He opened one and showed it to the girl. "Did she look like this?"

The girl stared at it. "Same hair, but I don't know for sure that was her, but I can't say it wasn't, either. I honestly couldn't tell you."

Dawson pocketed the phone and took out a card. "Thank you. If you remember anything else, please call me."

"Is she okay, sir?"

Confused, Dawson stared at her for a second. "Why would you ask if *she* was okay?"

"Well, I don't know...she left alone and well, the streets aren't always safe." She shrugged.

Dawson contemplated her words. "I don't know about her. But this man didn't make it home last night, and that is what we're trying to find the an-swers to."

The girl seemed surprised but didn't say another word. Dawson thanked her again and headed to the door.

twenty-two

Dawson walked the street in the cool, crisp air. Autumn had really started to set in, and early morning walks were one of his favorite things to do in the fall. The leaves had just started to change to a burnt orange, and the air had a crispness to it that invigorated his tired mind. His cases were wearing him down—brought on by the long hours and the horrendous nature of them, even though the current one seemed a bit less gory than some of the others he had dealt with in the recent past.

What was becoming of this area? Connecticut had always held a special place in his heart. He had settled there when he was discharged from the military, and he loved the seasons and the people there. Outsiders said New Englanders were rude, but they just didn't understand the brisk nature of them. They would do anything for anyone...

Just don't waste their time.

He smiled to himself and turned down the main street, heading for the coffee shop that had become a favorite for the locals.

He ordered his coffee and started back out to walk to the station. It was a good distance and gave him plenty of time to think. A niggling thought in the back of his mind hovered just out of reach—something just didn't set right with this case. Did it ever sit right with *any* of the odd cases he had dealt with in the past few years? Ali would tell him to open his mind and believe that all of his recent cases were linked to killers of the past.

Reincarnation.

That word had come up once or twice in every single case. Was it that he didn't believe? Or was it more that he couldn't wrap around his head to understand it? Could he believe in something and just not understand it? In his logical mind, no, that could not happen. But in the past few years, stranger things had occurred.

He knew it was time to call Sara again. The niggling he had *had* to be linked to Sara, and he wanted some answers. Deep in his gut, he still believed she was innocent, but why were there so many links to her? They needed to go through her past employment records and really dig through names. She wouldn't be happy that he wanted access to that stuff, but he needed to clear her name once and for all.

He pulled up her contact information on his phone and hit call.

"Hello," she sleepily said after a couple of rings.

"Are you sleeping still?"

She groaned through the phone. "Does it matter? I'm not now. What do you want, dear brother?"

He chuckled. "We need to talk. And I'd just as soon come to your place, if that's okay."

"Yeah, when were you thinking?" Sara's voice was

definitely more awake than when she answered him. He imagined her glancing around her room, thinking she needed to clean.

"I don't care what your place looks like..."

"Shut up, Wes. I'm not thinking that."

They were both laughing—even before she got the words out—which felt more normal than any interaction they had had since being reunited.

"You've got the address, right?" she broke in.

"Yup."

"Fine. Don't show up for at least thirty minutes to give me time to shower and wake up." She hung up before he could respond.

Whether she chose to use that name or not, she's definitely a Dawson.

He knew it would take him at least twenty minutes to walk to her place, so he took his time enjoying the weather and the warmth that had come over him just hearing his sister laugh.

Dawson arrived at Sara's place about twenty-five minutes after they had talked. She would just have to deal with him being five minutes early. He went to ring her doorbell, but the door flung open before he had the chance to push the button.

Sara grinned at him. "I knew you would be here five minutes early."

He shook his head. "You had no idea." He walked in and glanced around. Like he expected, the place was spotless.

She led the way into the living room and flopped onto the couch, pulling her legs crossed up beneath her. Dawson settled at the other end of the couch and kicked off his sneakers to get comfortable.

"I take it this is not really a social visit?" Sara asked.

Dawson shrugged. "Yes and no. I was dying to see where my big sis lived and since you haven't invited me over, figured I would invite myself." Sara threw a pillow at him. "And," he continued, "we do need to go through your records from your previous employer. I know you don't want to share names, but this will be between just you and me. I need some link between the victims and your previous employer, or it's going to look like *you* are the link."

Sara straightened. "So, is this a fishing expedition to see if I'm guilty?"

"No." Dawson nudged her with his foot. "It's an expedition to prove that I'm right and that you aren't involved."

Sara's eyes teared. "You truly believe me?"

He sat up and leaned toward her, reaching for her. She collapsed into his hug.

"I always knew you were innocent," he whispered. "I just let my anger at you shutting me out of your life make me act like a prick...wasn't that the word you used?"

Sara giggled. "You *were* being a prick."

Dawson pulled back. "Yup. Because that is who I am at times. But I am, and have always been, your biggest fan. You have to believe that that never changed."

Sara nodded. "Okay. Let me get the records. Everything is in log books, so it will take some time to go through it all. Table or floor?"

He laughed. "Floor to start, though if we stay there too long, you may be helping me up."

"And you are younger than me!" Sara called over her shoulder as she left the room.

He chuckled at the way she scoffed.

They spent the next few hours poring through the books. Dawson asked detailed questions on most of the clients, taking notes in a notebook that Sara provided for him. He found nothing concrete that linked Sara to the victims, which although he wouldn't say it to her, he was relieved. He did believe her to be innocent, but he also wasn't sure about the business and her involvement.

By the time they were done, Dawson had a list of three out of the four victims that were linked to the former employer, but only one tied to Sara. At present, the fourth victim didn't seem to be linked to either.

"There is one further thing I want to talk to you about," Dawson said as they stacked the books and stood up.

"What's that?"

He pulled out his phone and opened up a picture. "A waitress said that this person could have been the one who dined with our last victim."

Sara looked at it, and then up at him. "Are you serious?"

"I'm not saying I meant anything by it. I simply want your thoughts on it."

"We just said I know nothing about the fourth victim. I've never been to this particular restaurant, either alone or with any of my clients."

"What about your friends?"

Sara stared at him, confusion written all over her face. "My friends?"

"You do have friends, do you not?"

"Not really. This isn't a business where I just have friends hanging around. Evie is my only friend." Sara pointed at a picture over on the table.

Dawson walked over to look at it. There definitely was no mistaking either of them for the other. He turned back toward Sara. "I wasn't insinuating anything. I'm just trying to cross my T's and dot my I's."

Sara nodded. "I get it. I guess I'm just irritated that even one of these victims are linked to me."

He pulled her into a hug. "Let's plan to get together soon, just a social visit."

Sara gave him a squeeze before letting go. "I'd like that, especially if Ali will be there."

"My company alone is not good enough for you?"

"Of course." Sara punched him playfully. "But two of us can always gang up on you and oh, the joy that brings me."

twenty-three

Ali had been dreading this autopsy all day. Not because she didn't enjoy them, but this case was starting to give her a bad feeling. She prepped the body and the area, then put on some quiet music in the background to try and soothe her nerves. It would do no good for her to miss something because she was frazzled.

She started with her Y-incision and removed all the necessary parts to get to the stomach. Just as she suspected, the stomach lining had a red velvet appearance consistent with arsenic poisoning. She scraped under his fingernails and found nothing to indicate a scuffle. She dictated notes as she went through the body as a whole. As she sewed up the body and slid him back into the locker, she racked her brain to see any differences between the four victims. She was hard-pressed to come up with anything.

She sat at her desk and continued to look for information on Nannie Doss. Nothing new came up and she sat back in frustration. What the hell was she even looking for? They knew this was a possibility—that the killer was a reincarnate of Nannie Doss, or a possession, or maybe just a copycat killer—but what information did they really know that would be useful? She could feel Wes's frustration at night. He took these cases so personally and when the answers didn't come, it wore him down. Ali had begun to do the same thing and wondered when she stopped being able to compartmentalize these things.

Cheryl sat soaking up the sun. She had done a chakra cleanse and was just allowing herself to be open.

She closed her eyes and let the sun warm her face. A sudden pain struck her. Not a fierce physical pain per se, but she pushed on her abdomen as a slow radiating pain slid around her stomach. The pressure increased with flashes of Dawson doubled over with pain. She knew immediately it was a vision, but she could not determine whether it was happening now or in the future.

She slowly inhaled and exhaled even slower. It eased the pain, but the sight of Dawson didn't fade. He was in a restroom, holding onto a sink before turning toward the stall. When the door to the stall closed behind him, her vision cleared. This was the first time she had seen Dawson in one of her visions, and she instinctively knew this was related to the case. Was this an attempt on his life, or was she manifesting something else altogether?

She steadied her breathing and kept her eyes closed,

then placed a hand on her forehead, trying to open her third eye. She debated whether to call Dawson, but without any concrete evidence of when the vision was happening, she didn't think he would appreciate it. Then again, did he need to be warned, and would he take it seriously?

A few minutes passed, and no other visions came to her, so she opened her eyes and reached for her phone. She dialed Ali and hoped the girl would have more sense than Dawson.

"Hello?" Ali answered on the third ring.

"Ali. It's Cheryl Porter."

"Hi, Cheryl. What can do for you?" Ali's voice registered surprise.

"Well, I wasn't sure whether to call or not, and I didn't think Dawson would appreciate me calling. So, I figured you were the one I could leave information with."

"What is it?" Cheryl sensed the nervousness coming from Ali through the phone. "Did you see something happen to Sara?"

"No, not Sara. My vision was about Dawson. I saw him ill." Cheryl tried to soften her words. "Just sort of a stomach bug I think, but I don't know. With the murderer using poison, I thought you should know. Maybe they won't come after Dawson, maybe it was more metaphorical."

"O...kay." Ali drew out the word.

"I didn't want to say anything, but then I figured you might be better to determine if we should pass the information along." Cheryl felt a pang of guilt giving such news to Ali, knowing she would worry about him.

"You did the right thing. I'm not sure I'll pass it along right now, but it will be something to think about." Ali huffed a breath. "Do you think the murderer will go after Dawson?"

"I don't know. Like I said, it was a quick vision, and it may not mean anything."

"I appreciate the call, Cheryl. If you see anything else, please do not hesitate to let me or Dawson know." They said their goodbyes and hung up.

Cheryl sat there holding her phone and looking out the window. What she conveyed didn't seem as urgent as it had when she was seeing Dawson bent over with stomach pains. Had she done the right thing by calling Ali? She didn't need to give Dawson any ammunition to disbelieve any more than he already did.

She closed her eyes and sighed. Seeing visions was not all it was cracked up to be, especially when there were lives on the line.

twenty-four

Dawson studied the photos in front of him. He had them spread out on his kitchen table as he sipped his morning coffee. Saturday mornings, while this case was going on, were no longer quiet and relaxing with Ali. He was up, drinking way too much coffee, poring over statements and files. He sometimes wondered if his job would either wear him out mentally, or just downright kill him for all the coffee he drank.

He set his coffee cup aside, knowing it would be re-filled soon enough. He pulled the pictures closer, each one a photo of the different victims with notes on the back depicting time and place of death, as well as possible links. Thankfully, only one victim had Sara's name on it. The others did not, nor did they have links between them. Dawson's next step was to start background checks on all the wives, or fiancée, and see if he could find links between them. Wouldn't it just be easy to tie up if all the significant others were linked, and this was a round-robin murder where they made a pact to get rid of each other's husbands?

He sighed. Nothing would ever be that easy.

"Morning. You're up early." Ali stood leaning against the kitchen wall. He had no idea how long she'd been watching him. Her hair was up in a messy bun, and she wore sweats and an old t-shirt that she had stolen from him.

"Good morning. You are a bright spot this morning." He stood, walked over to her, and pulled her close for a kiss.

"How long have you been up?" she asked.

"Only a couple of hours." He shrugged. "Coffee?"

"I'll get it. You go ahead and go back to what you were doing. Refill?" She picked up his mug as she walked by the table.

"Yes, please." He watched her before he sat back down. "What are your plans today?"

She slid into the chair next to him, all the while looking at the photos. "I don't have any really. You need help?"

"I would say yes, but I'm not even sure what my next moves are. This killer seems to be one step ahead of us all the way. There are no links between victims." Dawson sat back, running his hand through his hair. He had not shaved in a couple of days, and the stubble had started to itch. He never had been one for the scruffy look.

"Maybe we need to step away," he suggested. "How about a walk on the beach this morning?"

"Sounds good to me, but can I finish my coffee first? Some of us haven't had a pot already."

He rolled his eyes. "For your information, this is only my second cup."

An hour later, they drove up to the beach and got out of the car. The tide was low but on its way to crawl back up the beach. They had hours before it would be covered with water in high tide. They slipped off their shoes and left them in the car, and then hand in hand, they strolled down the stairs onto the warm sand. They walked quietly, each lost in their own thoughts.

Dawson abruptly stopped and stared out to sea.

"What is it?" Ali asked.

"What if there is no method to the killer's choice of victims? What if it's completely random?"

"It could be." Ali tipped her head. "But wouldn't they be more random than this? Sure, there aren't any links that we have found between them yet, but they all are established business owners and good, prosperous businesses, too."

"True. But there was nothing in their financials that stood out. I'm thinking of looking into the wives to see if there is any link there."

Ali nodded. "I think that's a good idea. What other links could be possible? Locations, where did they all attend school, grow up?"

Dawson glanced at her. "Those could all be links, too, but so far, nothing like that has come up. We have their home towns, and there wasn't a connection. Agewise, they aren't all the same age so I don't think attending school together would be a possibility."

Ali smiled. "You always seem to do major brainstorming when you step away from it. Keep walking and see what else comes to you."

They started walking again. Dawson cleared his throat after a while but didn't say anything.

Ali squeezed his hand. "You okay?"

He grinned at her. "You make me nervous sometimes."

She pushed him away from her. "Oh, please. How is that possible?"

Dawson grabbed her and pulled her close. "Because sometimes there are things I just want to say to you, and then I'm not sure I should." He kissed her before she could reply.

They started walking again. Thankfully, Ali chose the moment to just be quiet. He wasn't sure what he wanted to say...well he did, but he doubted it was the right time.

They arrived at the end of the beach where a cluster of rocks sat. They climbed up and sat on a flat rock near the top. Ali snuggled close to him, looping her arm through his.

"You know you can tell me anything," she whispered.

He kissed the top of her head. "I know."

"But you would prefer not to right now."

He glanced down at her. Was she upset that he hadn't continued the conversation? Probably. *Don't women get upset at that stuff?* He sighed.

"I'm just not sure if it's the best time with everything going on with the case and Sara."

She looked up at him. "I'm not upset, Wes. You know it's okay if you don't want to talk about it. I will say this though, when *will* be the right time? Our lives are unpredictable, especially yours with the job you have. Right now, we are here in the moment, just you and me."

He nodded. "You're right." He turned and faced her. "We spend a lot of time together. You stay at my house at lot and I at yours not as much. I'm wondering if it would be better, or if you would want to..." He stumbled over his words. "...maybe we should just consolidate to one house."

Ali slightly narrowed her eyes. "Are you asking me to move in with you, Wesley Dawson?"

"Yes, I guess I am." He watched her, doing all he could to dive into her thoughts. He might be a grown man, but he suddenly felt like a schoolboy waiting for the girl he liked to check the *yes* box on the note he gave her.

"It's about time. I was beginning to think you would never be ready for that."

Dawson groaned. "God, woman, why didn't you say something?"

Ali giggled. "In all seriousness, though, my lease is up on my house in another couple of months. I was going to mention that to you and see if you were ready to do one place, or if you weren't at that spot yet, or ever."

"I'm there. Just move in with me." He turned back toward the sea.

twenty-five

Wes spent the next two hours with Ali at her place, packing up things and stuffing their cars with what they could fit into them. They would have to arrange for movers to get the rest of her furniture once they had rearranged Wes'ss stuff to make room. Ali feared Wes might be feeling like she was taking over.

Wes, on the other hand, had assured her that he would throw out whatever furniture she didn't want of his and to just bring hers along. She wasn't about to do that, but it reassured her that this would be a good move.

They finally unloaded their two cars and sat down with a cold beer.

A car door slammed, drawing their attention. A few moments later, the door opened. "Anyone home?" Sara called out.

"Grab a beer and join us in the living room!" Wes yelled.

"You're going to make her get her own beer?" Ali asked and took a sip.

"You can get up and get it for her. It's your house, too." Wes hmphed as Ali elbowed him in the ribs.

"No one needs to wait on me. I'm family," Sara said as she came in, beer in hand, and sat down. "What are you two up to?"

Ali looked up at Wes. He nodded at her.

"Just moving," Ali replied.

"Moving? Where?" Sara asked, looking around.

"I'm moving in. Your brother finally admits he needs me around."

Wes mocked indignant, his hand over his heart. "I don't need both of you ganging up on me now."

"Well, it's about time is all I can say," Sara said. "Now you need to put a ring on it, bro."

Ali widened her eyes at Sara, shocked that she would even say it.

Wes started laughing. "Are you kidding? Do you see that horrified look on her face? Ali's not ready for that."

"Me? After how long it took you to even bring it up today about moving in." Ali rolled her eyes. "But let's put you in the hot seat, Sara."

Sara choked on her beer. "Why me?"

Ali smiled slyly. "What's the deal with you? Do you need me to set you up on a date?"

"Set me up?" Sara's eyes narrowed. "Why would you even ask that?"

"Well, you were on a dating site," Wes pointed out.

"What is this? I stop over for a beer and just a chat, and now my lack of a love life is the conversation?"

Ali and Wes started laughing. "Talk about horrified..." Ali muttered between fits of laughter.

"Very funny, you two. God, you two were made for each other." Sara stuck out her tongue.

Wes got quiet. "You did say you would like someone in your life, though."

Sara nodded before standing up. She grabbed empty bottles and went to the kitchen, returning with a new round for each of them. "I know that you're unhappy with my job choice, Wes, and trust me, it wasn't my choice really, either. It's a life I fell into. But at this point, I know nothing else, and I don't have the education to do anything else that would pay as much."

"No one is talking about your job choice." Wes sat forward. "And for the record, I may not understand your choices, but you do not make me unhappy. Sara, I'm glad you're back in my life. And whatever is going on in your life, I'm here for support not judgment."

"Thank you, Wes. You don't know how much that means to me, you just saying that."

Ali sat back, simply taking in the exchange. They both had needed such honesty with each other. Ali had witnessed firsthand the guilt-ease in Wes since Sara had been thrust back into his life. Regardless of the circumstances, the Wes that worried day and night about her had started to fade into this new Wes who was forever joking with her and trying to make her smile, while still playing the protective brother. Sara may be older than him, but an outsider who didn't know them would think Wes was the big brother.

"I don't know about either of you, but I'm starved, and I know for a fact that there is no food in the house." Ali's words broke the tender moment.

"What are you talking about?" Wes turned toward her. "Didn't you just bring the contents of your fridge over here?"

"I did. But it's not a lot and nothing to really cook up. I'm thinking we should order a pizza."

Wes grinned. "Well, that's not healthy, but I'm not going to say no to that. Sara?"

"I'm in, as long as it has meat on it and extra cheese."

Ali shook her head. "You two are definitely related."

twenty-six

The weekend flew by. Dawson had helped Ali settle into *their* new home, and Sara had hung out with them. Dawson did wish he knew someone who would be good for Sara. He would love to see her happy, and it had nothing to do with her job, but if she got out of that business, that would thrill him.

The moment he got to work, he immediately sat down at his computer in the conference room and started ordering background checks on all the wives and the fiancée of the victims. He didn't know what he hoped to find, but he planned to dig until he found something.

He went back to the notes he had taken with the spouses/significant others. None of them seemed all that broken up about the death of their husbands, except Lucy Mercier. Though she *had* sent her husband to the hospital alone when he was sick while she continued to work.

The one that stuck out the most was Daniel Sawyer and his fiancée, Deb. Not only was Daniel cheating on his wife with some unknown person—who he supposedly broke up with—but then he went on a dating site that led him to having a date with Sara. Sara got a bad vibe, and she left. The missing link in that scenario was the mystery women he broke up with before meeting Sara. Was she the link that tied all the victims together?

Dawson sighed. They had received the text messages as evidence, but the number to the mystery person was still being researched. Cellphone companies never worked fast, even for the police.

He picked up his phone. If nothing else, he could bug the phone company and maybe then a fire would be lit to get some information.

He left another message, got up, and headed for the door. He needed to clear his head and hopefully a walk between crime scenes would give him something to go on. As he walked, he mentally went through everything he knew about the case. Arsenic wasn't as easy to get locally that was for sure, but there were places online where it could be ordered from overseas. He had no jurisdiction to request records, nor did he know where to start. He could take a few hours and make some phone calls to the companies overseas and see if they had had any recent orders to Connecticut, USA. Maybe that would give him a lead. It would be looking for a needle in a haystack, but at present, he really had no other leads to go on.

His phone rang just as he was turning the corner where the Brew House was located. "Dawson."

"Detective, you don't know me and I prefer to keep this quiet, but I think I saw the woman you may be looking for."

Dawson stopped walking. "What woman is that?" They had never mentioned it being a woman. "Well, I don't know for sure you are looking for a woman, but there was a strange incident at the dealership, and this person was acting funny. She left immediately after coming out of Mr. Mercier's office."

Dawson moved off the sidewalk to a bench outside of the coffee shop. "I'm listening."

"She was there shopping for a car, I suppose. I tend to people-watch so I notice things that most people wouldn't notice." She paused. "She never took off her sunglasses inside, which is why I figured I noticed her. I thought it was just odd. Everyone removes their sunglasses when they come in from outside. Otherwise, it's just too dark and you can't see well."

Dawson murmured in agreement, waiting for her to continue.

"Well, she was working with one of the younger salesmen, and then they went into Mr. Mercier's office. She sat in his office with her sunglasses still on. When he left the building, she got up and wandered around his office a bit. Once he came back, she got up and left."

"When she was wandering around his office, did she touch anything?"

"I couldn't really see. She had her back to the door and my husband came asking me questions, so I would glance over to her sporadically. I didn't constantly have my eye on her."

"Thank you, ma'am," Dawson said. "I appreciate your call. Can I take your name and number, in case I have more questions?"

"My husband won't like me getting involved. I don't think I should."

"I understand. I'm just thinking that we may want you to work with a sketch artist to see if we can get a picture so we have something to go on since you didn't get her name."

The woman hemmed and hawed a bit. "I'll speak with my husband, and then call you in a day or two if he thinks that will be okay." The woman hung up before Dawson could respond.

He sat there with his phone in his hand, thinking. They had a possible lead, but unless they could get a sketch of the person in question, it would do them no good. At least he felt like he had made some progress that day as far as attempting to do something. Spinning his wheels was not a trait that Dawson enjoyed, and with these types of cases, it seemed like he spun his wheels more than ever.

twenty-seven

A couple of days passed, and Dawson was pleasant-
ly surprised to get a phone call from his mysterious
witness again. "Detective, my husband says I can talk
with the sketch artist, but he wants us to meet just
that person somewhere. He doesn't want the station
knowing our names."

Dawson silently moaned. "We will make that work.
I have your phone number here on my phone. May I
give that to the sketch artist so he can set up a time to
meet with you?"

"Oh, my number came up on your phone. Dear, I
didn't even think of that."

"That's okay, ma'am. All I have is the number. Not
your name." Dawson wouldn't break that trust even
though he could probably find out who she was.

"That's fine then," she responded.

"I'll have him call you in a few hours. The sketch artist I use is Thomas Hardin."

They hung up and Dawson immediately called Thomas with the information. Thomas had promised to try and get it done that day and get it to Dawson ASAP.

Only a few hours passed, when Dawson received the text that Thomas had the picture of a woman in a blue scarf and sunglasses. Her features were cleverly disguised and Dawson didn't think it was much to go on. Something about the picture, though, troubled Dawson, but he couldn't put his finger on it. She looked so familiar. He immediately printed out a few copies, then pulled Brown into the conference room.

"It's not much to go on, but this is the sketch that Thomas Hardin drew from what he was told by a supposed witness that came forward. The witness said that this woman in the sketch was in Philip Mercier's office the day of his death. I'm sure there were a bunch of people in his office, but at this point it's as much as anything else we've got."

Brown took the photo and glanced up at Dawson quizzically. "She looks familiar, don't you think?"

"I did, but I can't place her. Can you?" Dawson watched Brown.

"I'm not sure. Maybe it will come to me. Do you want me to go by some of the other places of businesses of the victims and see if anyone recognizes her?"

"Yes, please." Brown turned and headed for the door with the photo. "And Brown, pray for a miracle!" Dawson called after him.

Brown headed for the third victim's place of business, Brew House. It was his favorite place, and he figured a good place to start so he could get some de-

poison

cent coffee at the same time. It wasn't as busy as usual when he walked in, and he hoped that they weren't hurting for business with the murder mess that had affected them. Deb was working behind the counter, and Brown placed his order.

He went to sit and wait for it. Deb herself brought the coffee over to him. "Officer, was there anything else you needed?"

He smiled. "Other than the best cup of coffee in this city?"

She eyed the picture on the table.

"Do you recognize this woman?" Brown handed the picture to her.

She slid into the chair across from him, carefully studying the photo. She looks familiar, but I don't know who she is. She's been in here a few times, but that doesn't mean anything because there are a lot of people who come in and out of here."

Brown nodded. "Well, it's a start."

"Who is she?"

"We don't know. Someone saw her talking with one of the other victims, and we don't know if she knew him, or is linked to the murders somehow. Until we can figure out who she is, we won't know."

Deb nodded. "Good luck, Officer. I wish I could be of more help." Brown picked up his coffee and headed for the door. He would go to Harpin Financial next, the first victim's place of business.

It was a stroll, but Brown didn't mind. He and Dawson had that in common. He had been thinking lately of taking Dawson up on applying to the State Police. He had learned a lot of from Dawson over the past couple of years and enjoyed the man's style. Brown had been holding back simply because he was always feeling discontented and being in Connecticut long term might not be the answer. However, on the flip side of that, would he be more content if he was in a different position? Brown sighed as he strolled along. There was never a dull moment in his mind.

He arrived a little later at Harpin Financial and found Sam Porter's assistant. She looked at the picture quickly. "Not sure I know her. He had a lot of women in and out of here that weren't his wife."

Brown sensed a bit of bitterness in her voice. "Were any of the women coming in and out of here more often than the others?"

She huffed. "There were a couple. I would say *she* was probably one of them..." She pointed at the photo. "But I honestly couldn't put a name to her."

Brown narrowed his eyes. "Couldn't or just won't?"

She gave him a sweet smile. "I would never refuse to help you, Officer. However, I wasn't privy to Mr. Porter's private life as much as some people like to think. I may have seen the women, but I didn't know names and certainly knew better than to ask. Mr. Porter had an expectation of my not really seeing anything that I shouldn't be. I adhered to that and turned the other way."

Brown nodded. He wasn't buying it, but he couldn't really press her beyond that. He would see what Dawson thought of it and maybe he would want to pay her a visit to try and get more information from her.

Brown turned and left the building. If this picture came from a witness at the dealership, then there really was no point in going there. They hadn't been in any contact with the fourth victim's place of business since he'd been found in an alley. Brown decided to visit that place next.

He triangulated the city and found himself in front of the trader's building. It was the home to various brokers. He knew Michael Sydney was a well-known stockbroker whose office was on the seventh floor of the building. He started in and a security guard stopped him at the desk. Brown pulled out his badge and asked for Michael Sydney's office.

"Sir, he no longer works here."

Brown smiled. "I am aware." He pulled out the picture. "Do you recognize this woman?"

The security guard looked at it and shook his head. "No, sir. You go right ahead up. You will want to talk to Sheila."

Brown thanked him and headed for the bank of elevators off to the side. He rode up alone and when the door opened, he stepped out into an office decorated in a black and white theme. It was understated. The waiting room furniture was black leather with accent pillows of white. The walls alternated between black and white, with various pictures hanging on them. The room had a sterile feel to it.

He approached the receptionist. "Is Sheila available?"

"May I tell her who is asking?"

Brown held up his badge. "Office Brown. I have a few questions regarding Michael Sydney."

She nodded and picked up the phone. She spoke quietly and Brown couldn't make out the words. "Please have a seat," she said after hanging up the phone. "Sheila will be out in a moment."

Brown wondered if *a moment* would truly be a moment, or if this was a stall tactic. He sat down on the couch and waited.

He hadn't been there long when a young woman came around the corner. She was tall, and her three-inch stilettoes only added to her height. She was dressed in a black suit and wore a white scarf around her neck. *Stick with the theme, apparently.*

"Can I help you, Officer Brown?" She held out her hand. "I'm Sheila McIntyre."

"Nice to meet you. I'd like a moment of your time to talk about Michael Sydney."

"Of course, right this way." She led him down a hall to a corner office. It had a spectacular view with floor-to-ceiling windows on two walls. "Please have a seat." She pointed at a pair of black leather chairs. Brown had never seen so much black furniture and realized he wasn't a fan. *At all.*

He pulled out the picture and handed it to her. "Is this someone you ever saw around this office?"

She glanced at it and handed it back. "We didn't get many visitors in here unless they were regular clients. I don't recognize her, but I rarely saw Michael. Our offices were on opposite sides of the building, and he kept to his side as I did. I live in my office pretty much. In this business you stay close to your computer and your phone."

Brown nodded. "What can you tell me about the type of person he was?"

"He was a hard-working person. He was happily married, but he was in the office for long hours."

"Didn't have any outside pursuits?"

Sheila eyed him in a way that Brown assumed she knew exactly what he was asking. "I really wouldn't know. Michael and I didn't socialize in the same circles."

Brown stood. "Thank you for your time."

It was nothing really, but did Dawson honestly expect him to find any information? Probably not if he had sent him out instead of doing it himself. Brown didn't care. He loved being in the inner circle of these murder cases. It definitely kept the days interesting.

Brown circled around back to the police station to find that Dawson had already left on another avenue he was pursuing. He pulled out his phone and texted Dawson. *No luck. Should I go to the dealership with this picture and see if anyone else recognizes her?*

Yes. You might find the salesman that helped her, Dawson replied.

Brown decided it was time to drive. If nothing else, he could at least look at some cars, too. His sixteen-year-old vehicle had close to 150,000 miles on it. He needed a new one, but he hated spending the money on a vehicle. Maybe he should buy a boat instead and live on that. He chuckled to himself on that one.

He arrived at the dealership. People were milling around, but there were not huge crowds as he imagined there had been on the day of the murder, considering they had been having a huge sale that day. He wandered in and started looking at the SUVs in the showroom. He swallowed back the obscenity that came to his lips when he saw the sticker price. Thankfully, he loved his car because even on his decent salary there wasn't going to be a new one anytime soon.

A middle-aged gentleman approached him within moments. "What can we get you into today?" The man spoke as if this was a joint decision. Brown had all he could do not to smirk at the guy. He never did like salesmen. They were too presumptuous and pushy for his taste.

"I'm really looking for some information." Brown pulled out his badge.

The man looked at it and sighed. "What kind of information?"

Brown showed him the picture. "Do you recognize this woman?"

The man brought it closer and stared. "I don't. Has she been here before?"

"I believe she was here the day of the big sale you were having, the day Mr. Mercier passed away."

"I don't recognize her, but I wasn't working that day. You can check at reception to see who *was* working then."

Brown nodded, taking the picture back. "Thanks." He headed for the receptionist and waited until she was off the phone. "Do you know who was working the day of Mr. Mercier's death?" Brown asked without any preamble.

Her head drew back in surprise by the question, but she seemed to recover quickly and smiled. "I think we already gave that information to the detective that was here."

Brown showed her his badge. "I'm here on behalf of the detective. What I need to know is if any of the sales people who were working that day are here now."

The girl checked her computer. "Davy is. He's over there. Other than that, no one else is on right now."

Brown thanked her and made his way over to the salesman. He was a young man, probably in his twenties. If there was a God, Brown prayed that this man would remember the woman.

"Davy, is it?" Brown asked and sat down across the desk from the young man.

"Yes, sir. What can I help you with?"

Brown put the picture on his desk. "Do you recognize this woman?"

Davy grinned. "Yes. I thought I was going to get a sale from her, but she left without buying anything."

Brown smiled. "You worked with her then?"

"Well, I started to, but she wanted to only talk to the manager, so I left her in the office of Mr. Mercier, Philip. He couldn't close the deal with her either."

"Okay. Do you remember a name?"

Davy shook his head. "It was the oddest thing. She never gave her name. She test-drove a car, but...." He lowered his voice. "I goofed. I was so focused on the sale that when she said she forgot her license, I let it go. I know I'm supposed to get a copy of the driver's license from everyone that test-drives a car."

"I don't care about that," Brown said. "However, what car did she test-drive?"

"The yellow convertible. And she looked good behind the wheel."

"But no name at all," Brown said. "Did she give you any information that would help us find out who she is?"

Davy frowned and his forehead crinkled. "I don't believe so. She seemed very keen on staying mysterious. Do you think she was involved in Philip's death?"

Brown shrugged. "She may have just seen something that could help us. Thank you for your time." Brown left.

He stared at his old car sitting in the lot looking pathetic as he walked toward it. He would have to break down eventually, and probably sooner than later, to get a new one, but for fuck sakes, the price of cars these days.

twenty-eight

Dawson had gotten news from Brown that although the salesperson recognized the picture, they had no information about who she was. And it still didn't prove she had anything to do with the murder. One step forward, two steps back. He was so sick of doing the cha-cha with these killers.

He pulled out his phone and sent the picture to Cheryl. Maybe she could give him some insight as to whether she had seen her or not in any of her visions. His willingness to ask her questions and for help proved his desperation. *This case is making me crazy.*

Within minutes his phone rang.

"That was fast," Dawson answered.

"You didn't expect me to take too long, did you?" Cheryl's voice boomed through the phone.

"Of course not. What's the word?"

Cheryl laughed. "Right to it. Okay, this is the person I saw in the vision, but it came in after the murder had already happened. And her face wasn't as clear as it is in this drawing."

"Do you have any idea who it might be?" Dawson tried to hold back his frustration. "I don't have a name. But I have a feeling it is someone you know."

"Dammit, Cheryl. You know that's not helpful," Dawson grumbled.

She laughed. "You know these things aren't a perfect process. Think about it though. Who do you know? Look at the picture, Wesley."

Dawson bit his tongue on the words that wanted to escape him. "I don't know."

"You will." Cheryl hung up without another word.

Dawson cussed under his breath and wanted to slam his fist into the wall next to him. Damn infuriating psychic. Why can't she just have answers for him instead of this nonsense?

He sat with the sketch in front of him. He stared and stared at it. There was something familiar about it, but he still couldn't put his finger on it. He focused in on the sunglasses. They were fairly generic with the mirrored coating so eyes couldn't be seen through them. Everyone had this type of glasses. The scarf was draped around the face so no discernable features could be seen other than high cheekbones. The lips were curled up a bit in a half smile.

He exhaled softly. It couldn't be. He grabbed the picture and headed out the door. He needed Ali's opinion. Maybe Cheryl was right. Dammit, that wasn't a thought he wanted to have, either.

He arrived at the medical examiner's office in record time. Ali wasn't in her office, which meant she probably was doing an autopsy. He never could get used to the environment in her building. The scent of death permeated around him. The sterility of the building gave him the creeps and he hated going there. And there he was way too often just because Ali worked there. The things he did for that woman. He chuckled to himself. She would kill him if she thought he hated her workplace this much.

He walked over to the autopsy room and looked through the glass pane. There she was, music playing, as she worked over a body, open in the torso. Her hair was up in the usual ponytail and she moved about to the music. He opened the door and walked in.

"Hey," he said slightly louder than the music.

She jumped. "I wasn't expecting you." She smiled. "Come on over."

Dawson glanced at the body and physically held back a shudder. "I think I'll stand over here."

Ali watched him and shook her head. "The body won't bite. I think he's beyond his biting days," she quipped.

Dawson grinned. "Very funny."

Ali draped a sheet over the body and took off her gloves. She walked over to Dawson. "You okay?"

"I think so. Can we step out so you can look at something?"

She nodded and they moved into the hallway. "I know you don't like being in the autopsy room. I would have met you in my office if you had let me know you were coming."

He nodded. "It was spur of the moment." He pulled out the picture. "Look at this picture and tell me your impressions."

Ali took the picture, gave Dawson a quizzical look, then stared at it. "I'm not sure what you're looking for."

"Just first impressions. Does it remind you of anyone?"

"Well, I mean..." she stammered, and Dawson could see recognition.

"Just say it."

"It kind of reminds me of Sara. She has those same glasses. I noticed them the other day when we went shopping. I only remember because the thought went through my mind that they were the type of glasses people wore when they wanted to be incognito, and she obviously does because of her job."

Dawson nodded. "I hoped that was the one thing you *wouldn't* say. What am I supposed to do? I didn't think she was involved. She said she wasn't at the dealership, but if a witness puts her there...has she been lying to me all along?"

"Don't jump to conclusions. You need to talk with her first. Do you want me to go with you?"

Dawson shook his head. "No, police business. I can separate the two things." He gave Ali a kiss. "Thank you."

"I'm not sure you really want to thank me for confirming what you were thinking, but you know I'm here for you."

Dawson nodded. He huffed and pulled out his phone. "I'll let you know how it goes!" he called over his shoulder as he was walking away.

I need to talk to you. Dawson sent the text to Sara and waited for the reply. He was going to her place whether she wanted him there or not. He dreaded the upcoming conversation.

He arrived within a few minutes. The outside door was open to the building and Dawson entered. He jogged up the stairs to the next level and knocked on Sara's door.

"She's not home," a young woman's voice said behind him.

He turned and saw a woman dressed in yoga pants and a sweatshirt. "Do you live in this building?"

The woman smiled. "No, I'm her friend, Evie. You must be the brother."

Dawson nodded. "Do you know where she is?"

Evie eyed him. "She sometimes goes for a run. I thought I would take the chance to see if she wanted to go to yoga with me. Obviously not."

Dawson stepped around her. "Thanks for the info." There was something about Sara's friend that was weird. If she knew Sara was running, why would she just stop by for yoga?

He started down the stairs, and then stopped at the door and looked back. Evie stood at the top of the stairs watching him. He held the door open and waited for her to join him. "She's obviously not here."

Evie came down the steps slowly and walked outside. "Should I tell her you stopped by?"

"She will know. I am sure I'll be talking with her soon."

Dawson watched Evie walk down the street toward a car—a red Toyota. After she got in the car, he focused in on the license plate, committing it to memory. Once she drove away, he jotted it down in his notes on his phone.

twenty-nine

Dawson returned to the station to find the background reports had come in. The one for Deborah Walker held very little information. She had lived a quiet life and didn't seem to run in the same circles as the other wives.

Now the other wives—interestingly enough—were all part of the elite class in the area. Dawson pored through each of them making notes on where they went to school, what jobs they had had, and what they seemed to be doing now. Ironically, all three of the wives of the victims: Cecilia Porter, Lucy Mercier, and Brianna Sydney, all worked on the board of a local charity. They were part of a gala that had their big annual fundraiser a month prior.

Dawson sat back and thought. None of them had mentioned the gala as being something they were a part of. Of course, his questioning hadn't gone that way, either.

This was an interesting turn of events. He pulled his computer closer and started to research the gala location and who had done the catering. It seemed like a good place to begin and see what he could find on the wives. Maybe he had been looking in the wrong direction all along—focusing on the victims' outside curricular activities as being the reason for the deaths. Maybe, just maybe, it was a little closer to home than he thought.

It would be very convenient that Cecilia Porter immediately pointed at Sara for her husband dying, considering Sara was involved with him. But that strengthened her own motive as a jilted spouse.

Dawson made a few notes to get him started, then closed his laptop, and headed for the door. Brown was just coming in. "Walk with me, Brown."

"Yes, si...Dawson," Brown stammered.

Dawson chuckled. That *sir* would trip Brown up for a while still, but at least he was trying. "I've got a lead we need to check out."

They rode in silence across the city into a district that Dawson didn't usually see too much. He parked and they walked up to the Convention Center where the gala had been held. It was empty when they walked in, eerily quiet.

They wandered around until a security guard approached them. "What can I do for you?"

Dawson showed his badge. "Detective Dawson, and this is Officer Brown. We'd like to speak to someone about the Children's Charity Gala that was here last month."

The security guard slowly bobbed his head as if in thought. "I'm not sure who to send you to. Most of the higher-ups aren't here. Their main office is across the street." He pointed out the door. "Third floor is the convention center offices."

"Thank you, sir." Dawson shook his hand.

Brown and Dawson jogged across the street and entered the building. They called for the elevator, and when it arrived at the third floor, they exited into a room that looked like a living room straight out of *Home and Gardens* magazine. It was homey, yet upscale. Dawson felt the warmth that oozed from the décor. He nodded in approval as they made their way to the receptionist.

"Detective Dawson," he said to the woman at the desk. "I'm looking to speak to someone who would have first-hand knowledge about the Children's Charity Gala and may have even been there that night."

"Teri was in charge of that event. Let me see if she is available." She picked up the phone and spoke quietly. When she hung up, she stood. "Right this way."

She led them back to an office where a young woman sat. She rose when she saw them. "Teri Lowen." She held out her hand.

"Detective Dawson. This is Officer Brown." Dawson shook her hand, as did Brown before they sat down.

"I understand you have some questions regarding the Children's Charity Gala. I was the lead on that event and was in attendance that night to make sure everything went smoothly."

"Who do you deal with directly on the board of that charity?"

"It varies from year to year. It depends on who is the chairperson for the event. The board rotates that position. This year it was a Cecilia Porter that I dealt with."

Dawson perked up. "Really? And how was she to work with?"

Teri smiled. "She was a handful. Had very specific details that she wanted followed to the T. She wasn't

E.L. Reed

exactly happy when any glitches came up, or if we recommended changing anything. Somethings just aren't capable of being done in an event like this. We have a lot of vendors we can use and can do a lot of things, but sometimes ideas can be a little out of reach. She didn't take it well if we suggested anything was out of reach."

"When you say she didn't take it well, did she lose her temper, or what do you mean?"

"I wouldn't say she has a temper, but she definitely is one that doesn't like to hear *no*, and she lets you know that she is in charge and anyone working with her needs to toe the line." Teri shrugged. "It was okay, and the event went off without a hitch. I did some creative problem solving."

"How was she that night?" Dawson asked.

"She was fine. She was a bit frazzled at the beginning, but that's not uncommon. She wanted everything to go off without a hitch, so it took her and hour or two to settle in and just enjoy herself."

"Did she enjoy herself?" Brown asked. Dawson nodded, loving that Brown jumped in with a question. He had wanted Brown there for his perspective on things as he heard the interview himself.

"She did. A little too much by the end of the night." Teri frowned. "Her husband died shortly after this event, didn't he?"

"Yes. We are investigating the murder."

"Murder?" She gasped. "I hadn't realized."

"Was her husband there that night?"

Teri nodded, her eyes wide. "They got into a bit of a row at the end of the evening. She had had a bit to drink. I'm not sure if he had, but she didn't like him dancing with another woman, so she started making a scene. Yelling at him, telling him karma was coming for him."

"Was there anyone else there? Did they leave together?"

166

Teri nibbled on her bottom lip. "I don't think they left together. I think he left right after the fight, and she went off with a couple of her friends."

"Do you know who the friends were?" Brown interjected.

"A couple of the other board members. I think one of them was named Bri—or something like that. I didn't know the other and didn't hear anyone mention her name."

Dawson stood and handed his card to her. "Thank you so much. If you think of anything else, please feel free to contact me."

She stood. "I'm glad I could help."

Dawson and Brown were silent as they made their way to Dawson's vehicle. Once they got inside the car, Dawson turned toward Brown. "Well, your thoughts?"

Brown looked straight out the windshield and was silent for a moment. "I think there is more to this than we originally thought. We could have a couple of other wives involved, and if they are the wives of other victims...could be a pact situation."

Dawson grinned. "My thoughts exactly."

"How do we play this?" Brown asked.

"I think the best way is to double-team the interviews. Do exactly what you did up there...interject when you want to ask something. We may hear different things, and we'll be able to compare notes. Shall we see if Mrs. Porter is home?"

thirty

Dawson and Brown pulled into Mrs. Cecilia Porter's driveway. The sprawling mansion looked gloomy and Dawson couldn't imagine living in something that seemed to have no personality. Dawson watched Brown take in the house as they walked up the steps to the front door. Brown eyed the place as if he was in as much awe of its enormity as the first time they'd been there.

They rang the doorbell and waited. Her nephew, Jason, answered the door again. "Detective Dawson. Was Aunt Cecilia expecting you?"

"Hello, Jason. No, she wasn't. I was hoping to catch her though."

"I'm hoping your visit means there's good news with you catching the killer."

Dawson didn't respond, and they followed him into the living room where Mrs. Porter sat reading the paper. She placed it on the coffee table when they entered the room.

"Detective Dawson and Officer Brown, what a surprise." Her voice sounded cordial, but not exactly friendly.

"We have some more questions for you," Dawson said.

He and Brown sat down when Jason gestured for them to take a seat.

"I suppose if you have more questions," Cecilia went on, "then you have not made the arrest that needed to be done, Detective." It was a statement, and her tone indicated utter disappointment.

"We do not have any concrete evidence to make an arrest at this point. We are following up on leads."

She made a disapproving face. "Well, what can I help you with beyond what I have already given you?"

Brown glanced over at Dawson, and he gave a tiny nod, allowing Brown to start them off. "Ma'am, can you tell us about the Children's Charity Gala that you were in charge of this year?"

She pursed her lips. "The gala? I can't imagine why that would be important." She gave Brown a bemused look and shrugged. "A rookie question. Good for you for starting somewhere."

Dawson bit his tongue and looked at Brown, hoping he conveyed a *brush it off* expression.

What a bitch.

"Well, the gala is an annual event that we do to raise money for the Children's Charity, which is a charity for less fortunate children. Our biggest recipient is the orphanage out on the West Side."

Brown looked at her straight in the eye. "That's great that you feel you can *help the less fortunate*. I'm more interested in the events that happened at the gala between you and Mr. Porter."

Dawson inwardly cheered. Brown was holding his own and Dawson couldn't have been prouder. And it became even sweeter when Cecilia Porter squirmed, actually *squirmed* in her chair.

"I don't know what you mean. The event went off without a problem. Everyone seemed to have a good time."

Dawson watched Cecilia, and then glanced at Jason. He was sitting extremely straight in his chair and Dawson couldn't tell if this seemed to be news to him or if he knew what they were referring to. "Jason, were you there that night?"

"No, sir," he answered, "I was out of town."

Brown looked at Dawson and Dawson gave him the *go ahead* nod again. Brown turned back to Cecilia. "And you and Mr. Porter did not have an argument that night in front of the guests?"

"I don't believe so. And honestly, I think you have a lot to learn regarding police work if you come here fishing, young man." Dawson could tell Cecilia was stalling, and he knew Brown could also.

Brown deadpanned. "Oh, ma'am, I never fish."

Her face reddened, and she turned to Dawson. "Detective, please. If you find this line of questioning acceptable, I will need to call your boss."

"Would you prefer we continue the questioning at the station?" Dawson asked. "We have it on good authority that there was an argument. It would save a lot of time, and honestly, it would go far for you if you stopped stalling and just answered the question."

Cecilia started to stand, and Jason put a hand on her arm. "Auntie, answer the questions."

She sat back down. "Fine. Yes, Sam and I had an argument. I had had a bit too much to drink and was

171

sick of seeing him fawn over other women in front of me. I regret letting my anger get the better of me, but it wasn't anything that I would kill over."

"Where do you draw the line?" Dawson asked.

"That is not what I meant," Cecilia protested.

Brown smirked. "Who were the women that rallied around you after the argument?"

"Women?" She seemed confused for a moment. "Oh, fellow board members."

"And their names?" Brown prompted.

Cecilia looked visibly uncomfortable. "Is it necessary for me to give you names? It was a private matter."

Dawson shook his head at Brown. "Mrs. Porter, you know the answer to that, especially when we know one of them is sitting in the same exact position as you."

"Meaning what?"

Dawson tilted his head as he looked at her. "A widow by murder."

"Lucy was there, but you don't think our husbands' murders are connected?"

Dawson hid his shock. "Lucy Mercier?"

"Yes, isn't that who you meant?"

"No. I was talking about Brianna Sydney."

Cecilia's hand came to her throat and she shuddered. "I didn't know Michael had been killed. I knew he died, but she didn't say it was murder."

"Doesn't it seem a bit coincidental that all three of you have lost your husbands in the same fashion within weeks of each other?" Dawson asked.

She nodded slowly but did not reply.

thirty-one

Dawson turned the car out of the Porter's driveway. "Who do you think she will call first to warn?"

"I'm guessing Lucy Mercier," Brown replied.

"Good. Then let's go see Brianna Sydney." Dawson drove in silence for a while. "By the way, good job holding your own against that bitch. You didn't let her faze you at all."

"Thank you. People like that piss me off. I tried to stay cool, but damn, I just wanted to tell her off. Do you think she's capable of murder?"

Dawson shrugged. "I think anyone is capable of murder under the right circumstances. The question is, was she pushed enough by her marital circumstances to kill her husband?"

Brown didn't respond but nodded. They arrived at the Sydney's home shortly, and Brown whistled as they drove up to the front of the place. "These people are all in the *more money than God* boat."

Dawson laughed. "You got that right. They didn't marry a police officer."

"True that."

The door opened just as they were ascending the steps. "Detective, I was expecting you."

Dawson raised an eyebrow. "Get a call from Cecilia? That was quick. I figured she would call Lucy first."

Brianna blushed. "I don't know what she told you, but we aren't really that friendly. We serve on the board together for the charity." She gestured for them to follow her.

They walked down a long hallway into the kitchen, where she led them through the back door and out onto the patio. She made her way off to the side and indicated a table with an umbrella. Brown and Dawson took seats at the table, and Brianna sat across from them.

"Cecilia just called and reamed me out because I didn't tell her Michael was murdered. Honestly, it wasn't any of her business how he died. Like I said, we aren't that close, and I didn't feel it was something I wanted to talk to her about."

Dawson nodded. "You were at the gala?"

"Yes, that was an awkward evening. Cecilia had a lot to drink. She could hardly stand up, and then she started a fight with Sam. It was just embarrassing to witness it."

"She didn't leave with him?" Brown asked.

"No, she didn't. Lucy and I took her to the ladies' room to see if we could calm her down. When we came out, Sam had already left. Lucy ordered her some coffee, and we sat with her while she had a cup. Lucy eventually said she would drive her home after she got another cup of coffee into her. I left before they did."

Brown looked at Dawson, and Dawson wasted no

time proceeding with the questions. "Why didn't you tell me that you served on the board with Cecilia and Lucy? Especially knowing all of your husbands had been poisoned?"

She shrugged. "I don't know. I honestly didn't think of it. And I don't really run in the same circles those ladies do. I'm new to the board this year, and it was Michael who wanted me to get involved. I hadn't met either Lucy or Cecilia until I was placed on the charity board with them."

"Do you know if the two of them have known each other a long time?"

Brianna sat in thought for a moment. "I don't know for sure, but they seem very chummy. I would have thought they were best friends the way they talk to each other."

Dawson stood and Brown followed suit. "Thank you for your time and your help," Dawson said.

"Of course." She got to her feet and walked them out. As they arrived at the front door, Brianna placed a hand on Dawson's arm, stopping him. "I'm assuming with all these questions, you feel that all these murders are connected."

Dawson nodded. "At this time, I have to assume they are. It's the same pattern. I'll keep you posted."

He glanced at his watch as he and Brown got in the car. "How about we reconvene tomorrow and go visit Mrs. Mercier?"

"Sounds good to me."

Dawson dropped Brown off at the station and headed for home. *Home.* Funny how now that it was Ali's home, too, he was anxious to get there at night. There was no point working late when he just wanted to go home and talk with her. She would be his sounding board, like she always had been, but now it had an even more of an intimate level to it. Dawson smiled to himself.

thirty-two

Dawson and Brown met at the station in the morning. They sat and had coffee in the conference room.

"Do you think Brianna Sydney has anything to hide?" Brown asked.

Dawson sat back. "I don't think so. I think she was pretty forthcoming, and if she doesn't really know the other two...I do find it interesting that her impression was that Lucy and Cecilia were best friends."

Brown nodded. "I think there's more going on, but Lucy will probably be the key that gives us some insight."

Dawson looked at his watch. "Let's go to the dealership and see what she can tell us. If she's not there, then we'll head to her house."

The dealership had just opened when they arrived, and there were no customers around the showroom. There were a few cars in the service area. Dawson and Brown entered the showroom and headed for reception.

"Is Mrs. Mercier available?" Dawson asked.

"I'm sorry, sir. She's not in this morning. I believe she usually comes in around noon."

Dawson nodded. "Thanks."

They turned to leave.

"Guess it's her home," Dawson said, "which may be better anyway."

Brown grinned. "Oh, good. We can see what kind of obscenity she lives in."

Dawson shook his head but chuckled. "It's disgusting, isn't it? The amount of money people feel they need to show?"

The large house with white bricks seemed to glare in the sunlight as they drove up. They had no sooner stepped out of the vehicle when barking filled the air. Dawson looked around and realized it came from inside. They weren't in any danger of a dog coming from around the house and charging at them.

They made their way up the steps and across the front porch to the door. Dawson rang the doorbell and grimaced at the high-pitch annoying ring. "That will wake the dead, that's for sure."

It seemed like an eternity before the door opened. "Detective, what can I do for you?" Lucy Mercier stood with a cup of coffee in one hand. She wore yoga pants and a t-shirt. She definitely was not all made up like she was ready for work, more like she had just rolled out of bed a few moments before.

"We have some questions for you, Mrs. Mercier," Dawson answered. "May we come in?"

She didn't look too thrilled about letting them in, but after a brief hesitation, she stepped back so they could enter. "I take it you aren't here to say you caught my husband's killer." It was a statement, not a question.

"No, ma'am." Dawson followed her into a small den-like room. It had two chairs, and she took one of them. Dawson nodded for Brown to take the other as he stood against the doorframe.

"Well, what other questions could you possibly have for me?"

Brown raised an eyebrow to Dawson, to which Dawson nodded. "Ma'am," Brown started, "could you tell us about the gala? Specifically about the fight between Sam and Cecilia Porter?"

She scoffed. "Fight? Darling, that was no fight. Those two bickered constantly."

"Not exactly the way it has been portrayed to us, but please feel free to enlighten us." Brown sat back and motioned for her to continue.

"I have known those two most of my adult life. Cecilia has always been a difficult woman, liking things to be done a certain way. Sam wasn't one to be controlled. It caused rough seas between them at times. The night of the gala, Cecilia had a bit too much to drink, and she went off on him. It was nothing that most people in our circles haven't seen before."

"Seems a bit inappropriate to have an argument like that at a gala," Dawson interjected. "Especially if Cecilia is all about making sure things are done the right way."

"That is what happens when you have too much to drink." Lucy shrugged. "It happens to the best of us at times."

"Was your husband at the gala?" Brown asked.

"Philip was not. He had worked late, and then came home. Galas are not his thing...*were* not his thing."

"That didn't bother you?" Brown asked.

Lucy laughed. "No. Honestly, I preferred he not go

to things that didn't interest him. He was a pain in the ass if he was unhappy about doing something he didn't want to do. It was much more enjoyable for me if he wasn't there."

Dawson noticed some pictures off to the side on a bookcase, and he wandered over to look at them. "Who is this?" He picked up a picture that had a young Lucy with another young woman. Both had blue scarves draped around their heads like the sketch that had been done, both sporting sunglasses.

"That was me and Cecilia shortly after we became friends. We had gone away for a weekend. We had just bought the scarves and thought we looked like movie stars." She smiled as she related the memory.

"Thank you for your time," Dawson said as he put the picture back in place. "We appreciate it."

"I'm not sure exactly what it is you're looking for, Detective, but if it helps you find the killer, then I'm glad to be of service."

Brown didn't say a word all the way to the car. "What was all that about?" he asked the instant they were inside the vehicle with the doors closed.

"We weren't getting anything out of her. Cecilia had already primed her. However, that picture…"

"What about the picture?" Brown asked.

Dawson held out his phone to him. Brown had not seen him snap a photo of the picture, but he saw the two women now. Both identical to the sketch of the mystery woman they were looking for. "Do you think they were both involved?"

"I think it's a definite possibility and one to look further into."

thirty-three

Dawson picked up his phone. It had been a couple of days since he tried to meet with Sara, and he hadn't heard from her at all. Since lately he'd been hearing from her regularly, her silence worried him.

He had begun to wonder if the so-called witness was someone trying to throw him off the scent. The sketch did look like Sara, but he still didn't believe she was involved. Did he feel that way just because she was his sister, though? Was he trying hard to find other possibilities so he wouldn't have to see what was right in front of him?

He needed to clear the air with her regarding the sketch anyway, for nothing else but his due diligence for his job. He had thought about going to see her by himself, but now he considered taking Brown along. He could give him the sketch and Dawson could see what his thoughts were when he saw Sara. Dawson had begun to really trust Brown. He had a good head on his shoulders and an impressive gut instinct, which would take him far working in crime.

Meet me at the station. One more person to visit. Dawson sent the text and sat back to finish his coffee. He would get to the station and pick up Brown. He grabbed his phone to send one more message.

I'll be at your place in 30. Please be there. It's important.

He didn't wait very long before his phone pinged. *I'm home.* Short and sweet. His sister never minced words when she didn't have to.

He rinsed out his cup and headed to get Brown. He didn't want the upcoming encounter with Sara to be unpleasant, but he didn't want to give her a heads up about him bringing another officer with him. He braced himself for the aftermath of blindsiding her.

Dawson collected Brown, and they arrived at his sister's apartment within thirty minutes. Before they got out of the car, Dawson handed the picture to Brown. "I want you to look at this *carefully*. When I showed it to you the very first time, you told me that there was something familiar about it. Well, we're going upstairs to talk to my sister. The first suspect brought in on this case, Sara Wesley, is actually my sister. I need you to keep that tidbit to yourself. However, there are links between her and some of the victims. It's a long story, and I'll give you the information you need, but right now, I'm concerned that this sketch looks like my sister. I'm trying to be objective, and that's why you are here."

Brown nodded and didn't say a word. He focused in on the picture for a few moments, then looked up to Dawson and simply nodded. "Let's go."

Dawson breathed a sigh of relief. His job could be on the line if he was found hiding information regarding his sister, if in fact, she could be a suspect. He knew he could trust Brown. They climbed the stairs and the door flung open within seconds of his knock.

"What is this?" Sara asked as she let them in.

"*This* is Officer Brown. He's helping me with the murders." Dawson moved into the living room.

"Welcome, Officer Brown." Sara gestured for him to follow Dawson. "So, I assume you aren't here for a brotherly visit?"

Brown had the picture in his hand and was glancing at it while he watched Sara. Dawson kept trying to read his face, but Brown gave nothing away. "Sit, Sara, please."

Sara sat down on the couch and pointed at a chair. "Please, Officer Brown, have a seat." She turned her attention to Dawson.

"Do you have a blue scarf?" Officer Brown asked without hesitation.

Sara snapped her head in his direction.

Dawson faced him also, shocked that he would choose that as his first question. Brown merely shrugged at him.

"I do," Sara said, and her gaze went to the kitchen table—which both Dawson and Brown could see from where they were sitting. Dawson realized that Brown must have already seen it. There on the table were a pair of sunglasses and a blue scarf.

"Fuck," Dawson softly swore.

"What's going on, Wes?" Sara turned and faced him.

He searched her eyes and found only confusion, so he held his hand out for the picture from Brown. Brown passed it over. Dawson briefly glanced at it, then handed it to Sara.

183

Sara looked at it, shock registering on her face. "You think this is me?"

"You have to admit it looks like you," Brown said before Dawson could answer.

She looked at him and nodded. "Yes, but where did you get this?"

Dawson was grateful Brown took over. He didn't have the words, and he needed to just see what his sister's body language conveyed.

"A witness came forward and said this person..." Brown pointed to the picture, "was at the dealership when Philip Mercier was murdered."

"*I* wasn't at the dealership. I have *never* been there." Sara's voice rose an octave in panic.

Brown sat forward in the chair. "Sara, we have to follow all leads...viable or not."

"Does that mean you don't think this is a viable lead?" Her eyes pleaded with Brown, and then she looked at Dawson. "You don't think this is me, do you?"

"No, I don't, Sara. But you have to admit it looks like you," Dawson wearily said.

"And I have a blue scarf and sunglasses right there on my table." She went over and grabbed both of them. "And the glasses are the same shape and everything."

Brown stood and took them from her in one hand. With his free hand, he took her hand. "Sara, Ms. Wesley, deep breath. We aren't here accusing you of anything."

She squeezed his hand. "Thank you. Please, call me Sara."

"Talk this through with me." Brown didn't let go of her hand, and they sat down on the couch together, Sara between Brown and Dawson. Dawson couldn't be more grateful for the way Brown was handling the situation.

"Through what exactly?" Sara asked.

"I haven't updated Brown on anything, Sara," Dawson broke in.

Sara nodded. "You were keeping it all a secret just because I'm your sister."

"I don't believe you are a suspect," Dawson said, then caught Brown's eye and gave an apologetic look. "I didn't mean to bring you into this mess, Brown."

Brown shook his head. "Look, we're in this. If Dawson thinks you're innocent, I trust that. So, let's talk through this, but I need you to give me all the information."

Sara nodded and sighed. "Well..." She glanced at Dawson, and he dipped his head, encouraging her to continue. "I have an escort business. Sam Porter was one of my clients, which is why he was found at my place. We were supposed to go to a work event of his that night, but when he showed up, he wasn't feeling well. Well, you know how that turned out. Then..." Her breath hitched as she wrapped her hair around her finger.

"It's okay. Just keep going," Brown prodded. He was still holding her other hand.

"Then I had this date with a guy named Sawyer. I met him through a dating app. I know it's weird, I run an escort service, but I wanted to date."

"Not weird," Brown interjected. "We all want to separate our business and personal lives."

Sara smiled thankfully. "I met this guy. He somehow knew about my business, and I left him there in the club. Wes told me the next day that he had been another victim. But I didn't know the other victims."

Brown let go of her hand and stood. He started pacing across the living room. "Okay, so you have a connection to two out of the four. We don't know who this witness was, right, Dawson?"

"No, they wanted to be anonymous. Where are your thoughts going?"

Brown stopped pacing and looked at him. "Where are the most obvious leads pointing?"

"Me," Sara said, and Dawson nodded.

"Maybe the obvious isn't where we should be looking." Brown smiled. "We have new leads that take us away from Sara, and I think *that's* where we need to be looking."

Dawson stood. "You aren't saying that because of the mess that this is?"

Brown shook his head. "Not at all. Though it definitely is a mess and you keeping it secret isn't going to look good if it comes out. No offense, boss."

Dawson rolled his eyes. "Sir, boss...knock it off. I know it won't look good, but I didn't know what else to do. If I removed myself from the case because of conflict of interest, who knows what would have happened."

"I agree," Brown said. "We just have to figure it out before anyone learns about this link to Sara."

Sara stood and walked toward Brown. "Why would you help me?"

Brown shrugged. "Simple. If Dawson trusts you, then I do also. I have no reason not to. Just don't break that trust."

Dawson sat back down. "There's more."

Sara turned toward him, shaking her head. "It's not relevant."

Brown glanced between Dawson and Sara. "No secrets." Sara sighed and left the room. She returned with the ledgers and notebooks in her arms. Brown rushed to help her with them. "What's all this?"

"Former secrets and names of people that you probably shouldn't know about. These were my former boss's records. Everyone she ever knew that hired us, that wanted to hire us and she rejected, or ones she approached and they rejected her. When she died, I kind of took all her records."

"Damn. Are you running her business to the full extent she was?" Brown asked as he started opening up the ledgers.

"No, not at all. I only kept the names of people I had worked with personally. I contacted a few others, but that was it. My circle of clients is very small, but they paid enough to keep me comfortable." She handed Brown the notes Dawson and she had made the last time he was there.

Brown looked at him. "What do you make of all this? If Sara wasn't your sister, what would have been your gut instinct to do?"

"I would have hauled her into the station for questioning and confiscated all this stuff for evidence."

Sara looked at Dawson in wide-eyed horror. He shrugged. "You said it yourself that first day, I *am* a prick at times."

"The point is," Brown interrupted, "you haven't followed through on that because you didn't really believe she was guilty, or did you do it strictly because she was your sister?"

Dawson felt Sara's eyes on him and he refused to look at her. "At first, because she was my sister. I didn't know if she was innocent or guilty. I hadn't talked to her in years."

"Wait, what?" Brown asked.

"We hadn't spoken in years. I had been searching for her, but when she was at the station that first night, that was the first time we had spoken since she left home."

Brown looked at Sara, and she nodded. "It's true. It wasn't the best way to reunite."

Brown pinched the bridge of his nose. "This just gets more complicated."

thirty-four

Brown hadn't said much when they left Sara's. Dawson kept waiting for the questions to start, but they rode in silence.

"Why did you bring me into this now?" Brown finally said when they had almost reached the station.

The question surprised Dawson. "What do you mean?"

"Why are you trusting me now?" Brown reiterated.

"*Trust.* I trust you. You have proved yourself in this case, and while I wanted to keep Sara and this part of my life separate from work, I needed someone who could be objective."

Brown nodded. "I appreciate the fact that you trust me. But I do have to ask—are you expecting me to keep this to myself if it is relevant to the case? I just need to know what your expectations are."

Dawson smiled. "You've come a long way from being that quiet, shy officer when we met on the hatchet case. I expect you'll do what you feel is right. I would never ask you to keep something of relevancy to the case a secret. I have too much respect for you as a colleague to do that."

"I appreciate that. I can assure you if it isn't relevant, it's safe with me. I can't knowingly keep something a secret, though, if it helps catch the killer. And for the record..." Brown held up a hand before Dawson could say anything. "I don't think Sara is guilty, either."

Dawson nodded, not trusting his voice to speak.

Brown snickered. "And she is cute."

Dawson gave him a withering look. "Back off, Brown."

Laughter filled the car as they pulled into the station. With a new perspective, they went to the conference room and started looking at their notes and the victimology board.

"I still think we need to talk to more people about the gala event," Dawson said. "I feel like there's more to the argument between the Porters than what has been told to us, especially knowing Cecilia called her two friends before we could talk to them."

"I agree. Caterers?"

Dawson nodded. "Yes, they would be the next logical people. I hate to ask for a list of attendees and contact them." The thought of the extra phone calls that would probably reveal nothing seemed like an illogical move.

"Well, hopefully we can get some answers from caterers and staff," Brown replied. "People ignore waitstaff, so they tend to see more and hear more."

Dawson pulled out the caterer information. He dialed their number and left a message on the voicemail asking for a list of names and contact information for any staff that had been working during the gala. Hopefully by the next day, it would be available.

"I need a step back from all this," Dawson said. "Let's call it a day and reconvene tomorrow. Hopefully, I will have heard from the catering company and we can start interviews with them."

"Sounds good to me." Brown stood. "Don't be too hard on your sister."

Dawson looked up at him. "I'm not."

Brown left the station and headed toward Brew House. He had a lot to think about. He grabbed a cup of coffee and went to a quiet table in the corner that was near the window. He loved to watch people from that vantage point, and it always gave him a good chance to just clear his mind and think through stuff.

It didn't surprise him that Dawson had held back on the information regarding his sister. Brown wondered whether the estrangement had been mutual or one-sided. Sara was a good-looking woman, but the escort business wasn't an easy thing to look past, especially with a police detective for a brother. Wasn't really Brown's business, but he couldn't help being curious. He admired Dawson and never thought about his personal life much. He knew he was involved with the medical examiner, but beyond that Dawson was a very private person and his private life was just that...private.

Brown didn't blame him. He never talked about his own private life with any of his colleagues. He often wondered if he really wasn't cut out to be a police officer. It never had been a job that he wanted to do when he was younger. He got into it more out of rebellion and trying to piss off his family. He thought it would be the quickest way to get them out of his life.

He tried to change his thought path, but memories of his own past kept creeping into his mind. Before the ruminating fully overtook him, he noticed Sara walking toward the coffee shop. He kept watching, and she came in and ordered. Once she had her coffee, she turned, surveyed open tables, and saw him. He pointed at the open chair across from him, and she nodded.

"You haven't had enough of me today?" she asked as she pulled out the chair.

"Nah. Don't know you well enough to feel that way. Just came to get some coffee and think about things."

"I'm sorry Wes put you in a bad spot."

Brown shook his head. "He didn't. I was a bit surprised, I guess, to be brought into his inner circle. He's very private at work when it comes to his personal life. And I'm not part of the State Department so we only work sporadically together."

"Ahh, that makes sense. But still, it must have been a bit of a shock."

Brown shrugged. "You see a lot in this job. I don't think much shocks me anymore."

"Have you always wanted to be a cop?"

Brown laughed. "You must be a mind reader. I was just thinking about that when you walked in. No, I didn't always want to be a cop."

Sara sat forward. "Sounds like there's a story there."

Brown nodded. "Yes, but I'm not sure I'm ready to share that."

"Fair enough."

"Your brother has been wanting me to apply to the State Police so I can work more with him."

Sara pursed her lips. "Is that what you want?" She took a sip of her coffee and looked right at him over the rim of her cup.

"I don't know. I love working with your brother. He's brilliant at what he does, but I'm not sure I want that kind of stress in my life. He takes a lot on his shoulders when he's solving cases...and usually it doesn't involve family. Imagine the load he is carrying on this case—and I don't say that to try and make you feel bad."

Sara nodded. "I get it. Even as a child, Wes wanted to save the world. He would take on everyone's problems and try to solve them."

"That's what makes him a good detective. I don't think I ever had that call to take on others' problems." Brown shrugged.

"Something must have pulled you to the force?"

"You still want that story?" Brown asked.

Sara smiled and turned her palms up. "What can I say? I'm an inquisitive person."

"I can see that. But you realize I can be very inquisitive also. And I'm thinking I would like to know what you were like as a child that made you turn to your profession."

Sara sighed. "You already know more about me than I know about you, Officer Brown."

"True. And can we skip the Officer Brown? I'm Kyle."

"Kyle, nice to meet you." Sara winked. "I'm not sure you look like a Kyle."

He started laughing, his heart increasing in rate just a fraction at the playfulness. "And what exactly does a Kyle look like?"

She coyly bit her lower lip. "I'm not really sure, more...How do I say this without offending you...?"

"Offend away." He mentally groaned. She could be trouble if he didn't watch it, but somehow he wanted her to be *trouble* with him.

"More put together. More of a sophisticated, more money type of person."

Brown laughed. "I'm not sophisticated enough for you?"

"That's not what I said at all."

"I know. I came from a rough neighborhood growing up. Maybe my mom was hoping by giving me the name, Kyle, I would break out of the family mold and become more sophisticated."

Sara grew serious. "I don't want to pry, Kyle."

"You're not. Let's just say the family business was not something I wanted to go into."

Sara nodded. "It's funny how sometimes our family dynamics really push us into something we may not truly want to do."

"Is that what happened with you?"

"Let's just say I ran away from home because my parents were so controlling, and then got into a situation where my boyfriend started pimping me out. I ended up in a job I'm in because of those years with him and living on the streets."

Brown nodded. "You know it's never too late to change professions. I'm not saying there is anything wrong with what you do."

"That's sweet to say, but let's be honest, most people aren't going to want to date or have a serious relationship with a girl who runs an escort business."

"Is that what you truly want, to have a relationship?"

Sara teared up. "Yeah. I want a family of my own, but I honestly don't see it happening. And I've accepted that."

Brown shook his head. "Don't be so quick to give up on your dreams, Sara. You have time and support from friends and family to change if you want to."

She smiled. "Thanks. Not to change the subject, but is this part of your investigation?"

"Talking with you? Not at all." Brown frowned.

"Do you think what we talk about, I'm going to go back and tell Dawson?"

"No, of course not. But I know my brother works all hours when he's on a case, and I didn't know where you were at."

"Well, I'm here drinking coffee—was thinking about the case and what directions I needed to go in—but then in walked a beautiful woman who was willing to sit and chat with me. As far as I'm concerned, in this moment, the case isn't even utmost in my mind."

Sara grinned. "I'll take that as a compliment."

thirty-five

Dawson entered the station ready to go. He woke up that morning with an email from the catering company that listed all employees working the day of the gala and their contact numbers. He arrived at the conference room to find Brown already there tapping away on his laptop.

"What are you working on?" Dawson asked.

"Just catching up on emails. Got something for me to do?"

Dawson gave an evil grin. "Do I ever!"

"Not sure I like the sound of that, but bring it on."

Dawson had printed out the list of people to contact, and he had divided it into two lists. He handed one to Brown. "Divide and conquer. I would just call and see if they can answer questions over the phone. I'd rather get this done quickly and hopefully, get something that we can really work on today."

Brown nodded and grabbed the sheet. He got up and moved toward the door. "I'll work next door so we both can have some quiet."

Dawson started dialing as soon as Brown closed the door. The first three people he called went straight to voicemail. He left a brief message asking them to call if they had worked the gala. He purposely made it vague, hoping that would entice them to call. He dialed the next number on the list—David Smith.

"Hello?" he answered on the second ring.

"Mr. Smith?"

"Yes, this is David. Who's this?"

"I'm Detective Dawson of the Connecticut State Police. Were you working at the gala a few weeks ago for the Children's Charity?"

"Yes, sir."

"I'm wondering if you saw anyone arguing during the gala?"

The young man laughed. "That seems like an odd thing someone would see at a rich gala. Those folks are as fake as they come." Dawson had to agree, but he waited to see if there was a yes or no to the question. There was a sigh on the other end. "Yes, I witnessed the argument of a husband and wife. I don't know their names, though she did call him Sam. Other than that, I don't know anything."

"I'm not sure that you don't know anything, since you saw what happened. I just need you to walk me through what was going on," Dawson prodded.

"They had both had a lot to drink. It sounded like the man was stepping out on her and she was mad. She threw a drink in his face."

Dawson straightened. "Do you remember what was being said?"

"Not verbatim, but the gist is he was stepping out and she was mad. She made some comment to him when she threw the drink at him that he would *get his*. She could hardly stand up, so I don't know if I would consider that a threat, though. Other than that, nothing else. Her girlfriends came running and pulled her away. They took her to another room or something. I didn't see them after that. After they took her away, the man called her a bitch and left. That's it."

"Thanks, David," Dawson said. "I appreciate your help."

They hung up and Dawson made notes. None of the wives had made mention that Cecilia had thrown a drink at Sam.

What a tangled web this is becoming.

He made the rest of his calls and no one had any other news. Some saw the same thing David did, others saw nothing. He got up and made his way over to where Brown had been sitting to make calls.

He waited while Brown finished up a call. "Anything?"

"Had a couple of people that saw the argument. There was a drink thrown. Other than that, nothing much...except..." Brown paused.

"Except?" Dawson sat down across from him.

"I had one girl that had gone in the restroom to check on Mrs. Porter."

"Really? And?"

Brown sat back. "She says she never spoke with her as Mrs. Porter and her friends were talking, and she listened for a minute, and then left."

"Did she hear anything good?"

Brown grinned. "Of course. She said she heard one of the women ask Mrs. Porter if there was any way they could *take care of this* for her. She said Mrs. Porter mentioned that if he was just out of her life, everything would be fine. Supposedly, she left at that point because she didn't want to hear any more and didn't want to get caught eavesdropping."

"Now that's interesting." Dawson crossed his arms. "Funny none of them mentioned that to us. Do you think we need to bring this girl in for further questioning?"

"I think if we want to talk to her again, we need to go to her and speak to her face to face. I don't think she'll offer anything up if we bring her here."

"Okay. I don't think we have anything to follow with the drink-throwing. I say we track this girl down and talk with her more, and then go have another talk with Cecilia—or maybe we divide and talk with Cecilia and Lucy at the same time."

"Bring all three in here at the same time, separate them, and go between the rooms," Brown suggested. "I would love to hear all three of their stories. I think we found the hole we were looking for."

Dawson closely watched him, and he looked relieved. "Brown, you realize that I had no intention of putting you in a bad spot, and I don't want you to feel you have to hold anything back."

"I don't. And you didn't put me in a bad spot. I'm glad you felt you could trust me. Sara really is a great person, and I want to be able to help her *and* you."

Dawson tilted his head and narrowed his eyes at Brown. "What do you mean, *Sara really is a great person?*"

Brown smiled. "It was a simple statement."

"Is there something you aren't telling me?" Dawson raised his eyebrow.

"That's rich, considering we are weeks into this case and I'm just finding things out."

Dawson grinned. "Where is that meek person who used to call me sir?"

"Ha. You created a monster because now I'm going to hold you accountable, *sir*." Brown stood. "Want some more coffee?"

"Yes, please. And I'm serious when I say *stay away from my sister*." Dawson casually watched Brown's face.

"She's a grown woman. And I'm not anywhere near her—other than a conversation last night." Brown left the room.

Dawson stood up and started after him, and then change directions to head to the conference room he was set up in. He needed to stop playing the protective brother, and certainly, Sara could do worse than Brown.

thirty-six

I sat in my car, watching her. She was running, which was her usual routine for the morning. I had been watching her for a while now, and she rarely deviated from it. So far, the police hadn't brought her in, which infuriated me. It had to be because her brother was leading the case. Maybe it was time to start pushing things further so her brother couldn't protect her.

I could leak some things to the detective's boss, but that may or may not get his sister arrested. And I actually enjoyed seeing her brother run around trying to protect her. I found it almost comical the way he was playing right into my hands.

I put the car in drive and started moving from

my position when she ran around the corner. It was time to check on some other small fires I had ignited. I glanced down at the vial sitting in my cupholder. It was never far from me. I had three vials left, and I didn't want to have to begin the process again. These were my last three attempts, and they couldn't be wasted.

I came around a corner and stopped abruptly. A delivery truck sat parked in the middle of the lane and created a backup of traffic. I watched as the man unloaded bags of linens and placed them on a dolly to get them into the building. Life had a way of placing things right in my lap when I needed them. My life had definitely taken a turn for the better, and once I got rid of Sara, things would improve even more.

I pulled into a parking spot and watched for the delivery man to come back out. Once he got in the truck, I moved back into traffic and followed him at a distance. He drove into a parking lot and shut off his truck. Looked like he intended to take a break.

I turned into the drive-through of a coffee shop next to the parking lot. "Medium, hot black coffee, please."

I paid and grabbed the coffee. Stopping just around the building, I poured the vial's contents into the coffee and put the cover back on. Then I drove around, pulled up to the truck, and rolled down my window.

"Hey."

The driver looked down. "What are you doing?" He acted suspicious, but he always had been.

"I just saw you here and thought I would buy you a coffee. A peace offering to say there are no hard feelings." I extended the cup.

"You didn't need to do that." He glanced around.

"Please. I feel bad about the way I acted the last time I saw you. I've been wanting to apologize for a while now, but when I saw your delivery truck and realized it was you, I figured it was the universe telling me it was time." I shook the coffee cup in my hand slightly to get his attention.

He reached out and grabbed it. "Thank you."

"No problem. And don't worry, you won't see me again. But I am sorry. I just wanted to wish you the best." I drove off before he could say anything.

My rear-view mirror gave me the perfect view as he watched me drive away and slowly took a sip of the coffee.

thirty-seven

Dawson had called Cecilia, Brianna, and Lucy and requested that they all visit the station so he could give them an update on what was going on—the best way to get them to the station. Upon their arrival, Brown and he would separate them and put them in their own interrogation rooms to talk to individually. That way, none of them could call the others and give a heads-up as to the conversation.

Dawson was ready, and he had given Brown the go-ahead to take the lead on the questioning since he had been the one who spoke to the girl. Brown looked like a kid in a candy shop. He had really grown into an exceptional officer, and Dawson planned to push him to take the detective test as soon as their current case was over.

It wasn't long before all three of the ladies walked in together. It surprised Dawson somewhat that they showed up together, but then again, was he really that shocked? He nodded at Brown and they both stood. "Come this way," Dawson said.

They led the women to the hallway of interrogation rooms. Brown opened door one. "Mrs. Porter, go ahead and have a seat and we will be right with you."

"What?" she asked. "Why I am being separated from the others?"

"There's just something we need to update that wouldn't be the same for all of you," Brown said. "Privacy reasons. I'm sure you understand." Before she could answer, he shut the door.

Dawson opened door two. "Mrs. Sydney?" She entered without a word, and he shut the door. Brown had already moved to the third door and opened it for Mrs. Mercier. With the doors closed, Brown and Dawson smiled. "Where do we start?"

"Let's go for the easy one first," Brown answered.

"Mrs. Sydney, the one who is out of the inner circle." Dawson grinned. "Let the games begin."

They entered the room, and Brianna was calmly sitting at the table. "What is the news, Detective?" She seemed almost too calm. Dawson hoped their plan didn't backfire on them.

"We've had some information come to light that we didn't previously know," Dawson said as he sat down. "And I'm wondering why you didn't bother to tell us."

Brown stood silently by the door.

"What information?" Her eyes narrowed.

"Well, we knew about the argument between Sam and Cecilia. But you conveniently forgot to tell us that you and Lucy asked if there was any way you could *take care of this* for her."

"Take care of what?" Brianna's voice shrilled. "What exactly are you implying, Detective?"

Dawson feigned shock. "I'm not implying anything. Did you or did you not, along with Lucy, one of you, ask what could be done to take care of *this* while talking to Cecilia after the argument?"

"I don't remember any comment or question being asked like that."

"Well, maybe you should run me through your conversation with Cecilia after the argument, when you took her into the bathroom," Dawson said.

"We just asked if she was okay. Lucy mentioned that she had had too much to drink and that she should know better, but other than that, there was nothing said about taking care of *this* or *that*, or anyone."

Dawson nodded. "Okay. Hold tight." He stood, and Brown preceded him out into the hallway.

"Do you think she's telling the truth?" Brown asked as soon as Dawson shut the door.

"I'm not sure," Dawson answered. "Something isn't right."

They moved to door three and entered to see Mrs. Mercier sitting at the table drumming her fingers as she waited.

"What is the meaning of this?" she demanded.

"We have a few more questions for you," Dawson said and stood to the side, allowing Brown to come in and sit at the table so that he could take the lead.

"Mrs. Mercier," Brown began, "could you walk us through your conversation with Brianna and Cecilia after the argument? I believe you had gone to the restroom to try and calm down Mrs. Porter."

Lucy glared at him. "What does our conversation have to do with anything?"

"Maybe nothing, maybe everything. Please proceed." Brown kept his reply cool.

"I don't remember what it was. We went to the restroom. We were just talking—telling her that she needed to calm down. I probably told her she had too much to drink. That was about it."

Brown tilted his gaze at her. "And no one mentioned taking care of the problem for her?"

"What? Of course not." Lucy's voice quieted.

"No?" Brown's tone indicated disbelief.

"I don't remember." Lucy's voice shook. "Why is this even coming up? Do you think one of us killed him? And then what about my husband, or Brianna's? Did we kill them all?"

Brown simply looked at her, expressionless.

She stood and started pacing. "This is ridiculous. I should call my lawyer."

Dawson stepped forward. "Do you need one?"

"No, but this is harassment. In fact, I *do* want my lawyer." Dawson nodded, and Brown and he left the room. Dawson called for another officer to get a phone so Mrs. Mercier could call her lawyer.

They then moved to door one. *This one should be interesting.* Dawson opened the door and proceeded in while Brown shut the door behind them.

"What is going on?" Cecilia's voice chilled the air. "It is unacceptable you have left me in this room for so long."

Dawson sat down and Brown took the chair next to him. They waited. Cecilia looked from one to the other before Dawson finally cleared his throat. "Mrs. Porter, it has come to our attention that there has been some conversation between you, Brianna Sydney, and Lucy Mercier about taking care of your problem, meaning Sam, your husband. Do you want to tell us about that conversation?"

"I'm not sure what you mean." Cecilia again looked between them.

"Well," Brown said, "after the argument, you were heard talking with your two friends. We were told that they asked you what they could do to take care of your problem, and I believe your response was, *if he was just out of your life, it would be fine.* Ring any bells?"

"I doubt it was said in the way you are implying, Officer." Cecilia leaned her elbows on the table. "You seem to be trying to fish for some information that you are apparently unsure about." She gave a small smirk before she sat back.

Dawson leaned forward. "Oh, we are *very* sure about the information we have. We're giving you an opportunity to explain it."

"If you have something to say, Detective, then by all means just come out and say it."

Dawson returned the smirk. "I believe Officer Brown came right out and said it. We are waiting for you to elaborate on that statement. If you choose not to, I'm happy to wait until you are ready to talk about it. But let's be clear, you will be staying right here until you cooperate."

She slammed her hand down on the table. "There was no conversation as you mentioned, and if you think you are going to keep me here, you have another think coming. Get me a phone. My lawyer will have something to say about that."

Dawson and Brown stood up and left the room. They directed the officer who had allowed Lucy to call for a lawyer to go ahead in the room with the phone to give Cecilia the same opportunity. They turned and headed back to Brianna's room. Surely, they would get their answers there.

She was still sitting at the table when they entered. Dawson sat down, ready to lay it all on the line. "Let's be honest, shall we? Neither of your friends want to be very helpful, and in fact, they're acting quite suspicious by being so closed-mouth. Where do you stand on wanting to help us catch a killer, your *husband's* killer?" Dawson held nothing back.

"I want to help you. I don't know what they're being closed-mouth about. Nothing happened. But again, I left before they did, so if there *was* something going on, I wasn't part of it."

Dawson smiled. "What can you tell me about Lucy and Cecilia's relationship?"

"They're close. I got the impression they had been friends for years. They are not two that I typically hang out with. I know them only through the board and this charity event that happened."

Dawson nodded, watching her closely. Her eyes never strayed from his, and she was forthcoming with information in a strong, confident voice. He didn't think she was lying. "Okay. You are free to go. But, please, Brianna, if you remember anything about that conversation that happened in the restroom after the argument between the Porters, I implore you to please contact me."

"Yes, sir. Of course. If Cecilia and Lucy had something to do with my husband's death, I want them put away for a long time. He did nothing to them, and I want no part of their clique." She stood and left the room before either Brown or Dawson could say another word.

thirty-eight

Dawson waited in the conference room for the lawyers to show up for Lucy Mercier and Cecilia Porter. He had no doubt that the two ladies would be walking out of there tonight. They had little to hold them on, and it was a long shot to think that even if they talked about doing away with Sam Porter that some evidence would just miraculously appear.

They had been hoping for a breakthrough, but were they just trying to manifest it without the evidence? Beyond a picture of both ladies in a blue scarf—which Sara had also, as did probably every other woman in America—they had nothing. In fact, they had more concrete stuff linking Sara to the murders than anything else.

Brown knocked on the door. "They're here."

Dawson stepped out of the room and both lawyers practically accosted him. "Was there something you needed to know from my client that didn't come out when you first asked her?" one of them scornfully said.

"There seem to be some details that were left out of answers that were given." Dawson shrugged. "That tends to make me a bit suspicious."

"Ridiculous," one lawyer muttered, scowling.

"Sounds like a fishing expedition," the other added.

Dawson smirked at them. "Brown, take these gentlemen to their clients. I'll follow shortly and talk with each of you."

Dawson stood against the door and watched them walk down the hall. It had been a long shot, but that play didn't pan out. Now, they had come to the dead end he feared.

"Sir?" a quiet voice said next to him.

Dawson turned to find an officer that he didn't recognize. "Yes?"

"I'm afraid there has been an accident, and I was told to ask you to come to the scene." He handed Dawson a sticky note with the address on it.

"I'll be right there. Let me just give my partner a message." Dawson moved toward Brown who stood between the two doors, waiting. "I've got a message to get to an accident. Can you finish up here?"

"Of course. I don't imagine they will be staying, but I'll go in and see if I can get any answers before they go."

"Keep me updated." Dawson turned and headed in the direction of his car. He found it strange that he was being called to an accident while in the middle of a murder investigation.

The coroner's van came into view as he pulled up to the accident. He ducked under the police tape and showed his badge to the officer who stepped in front of him to stop him. When the man moved aside, Dawson walked over to Ali. "What's going on?"

"Delivery driver seemed to get sick while he was driving, went across traffic, and hit the median," Ali explained. "He vomited all over himself and defecated a fair amount. He's dead."

"Why call me?"

"A hunch," Ali said. "Empty coffee cup, the vomit and defecation, I'm wondering if he hasn't been poisoned."

Dawson sighed. "And I had two suspects at the station when this happened. A fifth victim?"

Ali nodded. "I don't have any other information for you yet, regarding the man's death. But I thought you might want to look around—get any evidence before it just gets thrown away if people are thinking it was just an accident."

Dawson smiled at her. "Thanks. I appreciate it." He moved toward the vehicle where two officers were taking pictures of the scene. One of them approached him.

"The ME said to grab pictures of the inside. Said you would want the coffee cup for evidence to run trace-testing on."

"Yes, thank you," Dawson said. "Anything else you can tell me? Have you ID'd him yet?"

"Driver's license says Erik Masterson."

Dawson nodded. He peered inside the vehicle. It was a mess with the man still in the driver's seat, covered in his own sickness. Dawson held a hand over his mouth to not inhale the stench that permeated the cab of the truck. He moved around to the driver's side. He pulled on a pair of gloves and reached for the phone that was on the floor. It required a face ID, and he held the phone up to the man's face. It opened immediately. He briefly scrolled through text messages and found a short one to someone name Alyssa. The phone also had an email account that he wanted to go through.

"Evidence bag?" he called to the officer on the other side of the cab. The man reached through and handed it to Dawson. Dawson dropped the phone in the bag and closed it up. He also searched through the glove box of the truck.

"Okay to release the body, sir?" the officer called to him.

Dawson nodded. "Go ahead."

Ali turned when Dawson approached. "What do you think?

"It could be another victim," Dawson said. "I've grabbed the phone, and we'll send the coffee cup for arsenic testing. If he is a victim, he must have been drinking the coffee while he was driving. That would be a first, wouldn't it? He's lucky no other cars were in the way or we could have had other injuries or fatalities."

Ali nodded. "I was hoping we had seen the last of the killings, but I guess that was too good to be true. Do we know who he is yet?"

"Erik Masterson. I don't know anything beyond that. Do I need to call Sara to see if this is someone she knows?"

Ali looked at him. "You don't think she is involved. I thought you had ruled her out."

"I had, but the two suspects I had were in my custody when this happened so that kind of lets them off the hook. I don't think we're dealing with two different killers using the same method, do you?"

"No, probably not."

Dawson growled as he ran his hand over his face. "Just when I thought we were making progress, this happens."

Dawson's phone pinged and he pulled it from his pocket. *Nothing. They said they had no info and left with their lawyers.*

Thanks, Dawson replied. *Can you get in touch with Sara and see where she was today?*

What happened? Brown asked.

Another victim. Died while driving. No other info as yet.

Do we have an ID? Brown asked.

Erik Masterson

The exchanged ended, and once again, Dawson was thankful that he had found someone like Brown that he could trust.

thirty-nine

Brown didn't want to call Sara, so he drove over to her house. He rang her doorbell and prayed she was home alone. He hadn't thought to call before he came, but as he stood at her door, now he hoped she wasn't working. She swung the door open. She had never looked so beautiful as she did at that moment in yoga pants, an oversized sweatshirt, and her hair pulled up in a messy bun.

"Kyle, what a surprise." She widened the opening of the door so he could come in.

"I'm not interrupting anything, am I?"

"Yes, as a matter of fact you are. I was just getting ready to pop some popcorn and put in a movie. Care to join me?"

He smiled. "I'd love to, but I do need to talk to you first."

She rolled her eyes. "What now?"

"There's been another victim, Sara. Does the name Erik Masterson mean anything to you?"

She thought. "I don't think so. I mean, it sounds familiar, but I don't know why. He definitely isn't a work name." She shrugged.

Brown nodded. "Okay then. What movie are we watching?"

"Well, I don't really see you being a romantic, love-story guy..."

"Hey, I think I should be offended by that. I love a good rom-com if I'm watching it with the right person."

Sara laughed. "What's your go to?"

"Comedy or action, definitely."

"Me, too, actually. Action for sure. Do you like the John Wick movies?"

"Absolutely!" Brown enthusiastically answered as she went into the kitchen. He stood in the doorway watching her as she pulled down a bowl for the popcorn and starting making it. As it popped, she melted butter, and when the popcorn was done and in the bowl, she poured the butter over it, salted it, and shook it up. She grabbed a handful of napkins and a couple of beers from the fridge.

"Ready?"

He took the beers from her and followed her to the living room. They settled on the couch with the popcorn between them, and Sara turned on the TV and started *John Wick*. They munched on popcorn and watched the movie. When the popcorn was gone, Brown moved the bowl to the coffee table and Sara scooted a little closer to him. They both leaned toward each other and settled in for the rest of the movie.

His phone pinged just as the movie was ending. *Well?*

Shit. He had forgotten to text Dawson back and quickly typed: *She doesn't know him.*

"Little bro checking up on me?" Sara laughed.

"I forgot to tell him whether you knew the victim or not."

Sara leaned a bit to the side and studied him. "Did you come over here just to ask me that?"

"Well, I wanted to see you as opposed to call you." He smiled at her.

"Good answer." She moved back to a closer position.

Brown's phone pinged again, and then Sara's did, too. "Oy, guess he is not going to let this one go."

Brown looked at his cell. *We'll talk tomorrow. Get some rest tonight, tomorrow may be a long day.*

Yes, sir. Brown grinned as he sent his reply. He could picture Dawson rolling his eyes when he read it.

"He checking on you, too?" he asked Sara.

She nodded. "I suppose he means well. But if he's this concerned whether or not I know this new victim, I think he's still unsure about me being involved."

"Just trying to do his job, Sara. Give him a break."

"I know. I appreciate his concern, I do. But after years of not talking, it seems a bit overkill to me."

"He wants you to be safe," Brown said in a soft voice. "We both do."

Sara leaned against his shoulder. "Thank you."

His body tensed briefly before he slowly exhaled in an effort to relax. "I should go, though. Tomorrow could be a long day."

She sat up fully, replying to his comment without words. Brown had the urge to kiss her and hesitated before he stood. *Damn it. If she wasn't Dawson's sister, I'd have her in my arms this second.*

She watched him a second, then got to her feet and

walked him to the door. "Thank you for watching the movie with me," she said. "I enjoyed the company."

"I enjoyed it, too." Brown leaned forward and kissed her cheek. He squashed the urge to taste her lips, feel her tongue against his. He could feel the blood rushing to places it shouldn't be.

forty

Dawson arrived at the station early. He had tossed and turned most of the night, and then about four a.m., he got up and went to the station so he would stop bothering Ali. She would be doing the autopsy that day and needed the rest.

He found the station fairly quiet upon his arrival. Although there were officers on duty, it was a dead time of the day where shifts were just ending and beginning. Dawson liked this time of day best. No one really around to interrupt him, and he could get some thinking done.

He didn't know where Brown had been the previous night, and he was almost afraid to ask, since he was short on conversation. He had a feeling Brown had been with Sara, and he didn't want to pry. He was satisfied that Sara didn't know the name of the victim.

Dawson had been irritated with the notes Brown had left in his folder regarding Cecilia Porter and Lucy Mercier. The lawyers had advised both women against saying anything else and that was the end of it. They left with their attorneys, and now Dawson could only contact them via the lawyers. He felt like it was a dead end. But the unanswered questions regarding the conversation remained. It may have just been drunk women talking and no real meaning behind it.

Brown knocked on the doorframe as he walked in. "What's the word?"

Dawson glanced at his watch—five a.m. Apparently, Brown was an early riser like him. "Was Sara okay last night?"

"Yes."

Dawson laughed. "Okay. I assume you were there, but I'm not going to say anything."

Brown grinned. "You *can't* say anything. You are the younger brother, I believe."

"Don't even start." Dawson pointed a finger at him and narrowed his eyes. "She's probably too old for you anyway."

Brown laughed. "I like them older."

Dawson's concern took over, taking away all the humor in the conversation. "Not even funny, dude."

Brown just looked at him and Dawson let it go. *Damn.* It would not be easy to see his sister get involved with someone, especially knowing her profession.

"Her job doesn't define her, you know?" Brown said as if sensing Dawson's thoughts.

"Doesn't it bother you even a little?"

"Nope. I think we all have things in our past that we wish weren't there. It's where she goes in the future that will be important." Brown picked up the folder and opened it. "And don't read into that statement."

poison

They started going over the little information Dawson gleaned from the scene of the crime. They were
waiting on results from the autopsy and lab results on
the coffee cup as well as toxicology. Not much they
could do until that information came in.

"Have you tracked down any family for him?"
Brown asked.

"No. But I do have his cellphone where there was
a text to an Alyssa. It may be a girlfriend judging from
the tone of the text and the heart emojis."

"Still too early to call," Brown said looking at his
watch. "Damn. We both are early risers. How about
some breakfast?"

Dawson nodded. "What did you have in mind?"

"Sunrise Diner. It's just a few blocks over. Great
omelets."

"Sounds good."

They made their way to the diner in silence. After
they ordered, Dawson looked around to get a better
feel for the place. It was clean, well lit, and had all
kinds of baseball memorabilia on the walls.

Brown gestured toward the wall and had obviously
noticed him studying it. "The owner apparently used
to play for the minors. Never made it the majors but
has some great pictures of people he knew."

"It's a cool place. How did I never know about
this diner?"

The food was fabulous and Dawson couldn't wait
to bring Ali there. He frequently thought about their
first date in a diner when they were working on the
hatchet murders. Ali loved omelets.

She'll adore this place.

His phone rang, and when he glanced at it, it
showed Ali's name.

"Could you sense me thinking of you?" he answered.

"It better be *good* thoughts," she said, "since you left this morning without even a kiss goodbye."

"I didn't want to wake you. And yes, good thoughts. Brown brought me to this great diner. The omelets are to die for."

She laughed. "Bad pun, but I couldn't sleep after you left, so I came in early also. I'm done with the autopsy. Same findings. Arsenic killed him."

"Well, that was fast. I wasn't expecting anything from you until later today. Thank you."

"You can thank me with a meal at that place as soon as this is all over."

"You've got it."

"Talk to soon. Love you." She hung up before he could answer.

He turned his attention to Brown who he discovered smirking. Seemed he had been watching him with amusement. "Oh, whatever, Brown. Same autopsy results. Arsenic."

"Just sounded like it was more personal than the case." Laughter erupted from Brown.

"Last night," Dawson dryly said to put Brown's thoughts where they needed to be, "when I checked his phone, after I managed to unlock it, I took off the lock feature so we could get back into it. We should look at it again and see if there's something I missed."

"Other than heart emojis?" Brown asked.

Dawson ignored the remark, took out the phone, and went to the text messages. "As I told you earlier, the last text message he sent was to Alyssa. I assume she's his significant other as he ends the message with a heart and *love you*. Of course, she then responded with all kinds of the heart, love emojis stuff." Dawson rolled his eyes.

"And you said you haven't tracked down any actual family, right?"

poison

Dawson smiled. "Well, that is what *you* are supposed to be doing. See if you can find family for Erik Masterson. I'll keep going through his phone texts and emails."

Brown nodded. They worked in silence and found that the victim had no family around. His emergency contact was Alyssa Talbot—the presumed girlfriend. After Brown came to a dead end, they decided it was time to trace down Alyssa Talbot. Finding an address for her, they started for her apartment.

They pulled up in front of a nondescript building. Almost looked like an old store with an apartment above, but apparently the bottom had been gutted out and turned into a couple of apartments. Dawson rang the bell for Alyssa's.

The door slowly opened, and a young woman, who looked like she had spent the past few hours crying, stood on the other side of the doorframe. "Hello, can I help you?"

Dawson held up his badge. "Detective Dawson. This is Officer Brown. We are looking for Alyssa Talbot."

"That's me. Are you here about Erik?"

Dawson nodded. "Can we come in?"

Alyssa turned and walked into the apartment. Dawson and Brown followed her with Brown closing the door behind them. It was a small, one-bedroom apartment. The living room opened up as a single room with a small kitchenette. Two doors off to the right indicated a bathroom and a bedroom.

Alyssa sat down on the couch. Dawson and Brown took chairs. "Miss, how do you know Erik?" Dawson asked.

"He's my boyfriend. I was expecting him last night, but he never came home. He didn't call. I swore I wasn't going to be that girlfriend who called every two minutes, so I was waiting to hear from him this morning, but still nothing." Tears started flowing down her face again.

Dawson sighed. "Miss, Erik was in an accident last night. Unfortunately, he didn't make it and was pronounced dead at the scene."

Alyssa sobbed. "What happened?" she managed to ask.

Brown looked at Dawson. He reached for the box of tissues on the stand beside his chair and took it over to the crying girl. "Thank you," she whispered through her tears.

Brown sat down next to her, holding the box. Dawson's partner had good instincts. They both knew she'd likely need more than one tissue.

"It appears that he became ill," Dawson went on, "and his truck veered across the center line and into the median."

"And that killed him?" she asked. "How fast was he going?"

Dawson shook his head. "No, ma'am. It appears that he was poisoned. The evidence shows that he died before the truck struck the median."

"Poisoned?" The girl gulped for air. "I don't understand. Who would want to kill Erik?"

"We don't know. There have been a couple of other victims, and we're trying to find a connection to them."

"Who else?" She looked at Brown and blinked away more tears.

"At this time, we aren't at liberty to speak of the other victims," Brown answered, glancing at Dawson.

"How do you find a connection if I don't know whether or not I know them?" Alyssa demanded.

Dawson understood her frustration, but he had to maintain protocol. "There could be a connection just by the job he had in deliveries."

"He worked very specifically with upscale events. He wasn't just a delivery person to every Joe, Dick, and Harry. He delivered only to convention centers and such."

Dawson eagerly pulled out his notebook. "Do you know if he delivered to the convention center where the Children's Charity Gala was held a few weeks ago?"

She nodded as she reached for another tissue. "It was one of his regular stops."

"Thank you," Dawson said. "I think we found our connection."

"What about the body? When will I be able to plan a funeral? I need to call his parents—they're out in California." She rambled out the words as if her mind had finally started to grasp the situation.

Dawson handed her both his and Ali's cards. "You can call the medical examiner's office. It should be ready for release later today or tomorrow. If there is anything you feel I need to know later, please feel free to call me."

"Do you have someone you can call?" Brown interjected. "Someone who can come and be with you?"

She nodded. "My best friend lives next door. I'll text her to come over."

She sent a quick text, and then showed them to the door. As they were leaving, the neighbor came flying out of her apartment door and into Alyssa's.

forty-one

The air had a chill to it, especially with it being so early in the morning, which was extremely fitting for how I was currently feeling. There had been enough extraneous killings. It was time to go for the source. I had two vials left and each was specifically marked for two very special people. I sat at the counter and prepared the next to the last. This one would be fun, and I wished I could be a fly on the wall when I dropped off this very unique coffee.

I smiled as I put on my wig. Sunglasses next. I grinned at myself in the mirror. It was all coming together now.

I walked out the door and to the coffee store. It was perfect. I would slip in and out, and I doubted anyone would even notice me. No matter how observant some people were, they frequently never saw what was right in front of them.

Dawson yawned as he walked into the station. The nights seemed to get longer, blending with the days— sleep nonexistent at that point in the case. Thankfully, Ali was a trooper and not only fully understood the demands of the job, but she also supported Dawson more than he ever imagined any partner could. He started for the room he was set up in to look over files and double-checked notes he had made late the night before—or was it early that morning, before starting the day?

He noticed a coffee cup on his desk as he walked by.

Thought you could use this—S was written on the cup. He chuckled. Sara now sending notes to his work instead of his house. He never thought he would see that day.

He took a sip and continued to the conference room. He took another sip of coffee and placed it on the table as he moved around to study the victimology board up close. Five victims in total and no real link between them—except Sara. That still stung every time he thought of it. He had no real hard evidence his sister was involved, but Sara was connected to some of the victims in one way or another, yet not all of them. If not directly, then through her former employer.

Dawson leaned against the table, a cramp creeping along his abdomen. He shook his head. He really needed to lay off the coffee. This case was killing him from the inside with the amount of caffeine he was consuming as well as lack of a steady diet. He closed his eyes while he waited for the cramping to pass. He headed to his desk where a bottle of antacids waited for him.

He chewed a couple of tablets, then turned toward the coffee station where some bottled water was kept and swigged down a healthy swallow of the clear liquid. His stomach burned. He had just returned to the conference room when Ali appeared at the door.

"Hey, did you get any sleep last night? You look terrible."

Dawson glanced at her as another wave of stomach pains doubled him over. "Not feeling well."

Ali rushed to his side and held him up. "Have you eaten anything?"

Dawson shook his head. "Just a couple of sips of coffee this morning." He gestured to the coffee cup with Sara's note on it. Ali frowned as she looked at the cup.

"Are you sure that's from Sara?" Ali helped him sink into a chair, then ran to the door. "Get an ambulance!" she yelled out to the nearest officer.

"I don't need an ambulance," Dawson grumbled. Another pain struck. He stood and bolted from the room, heading toward the restroom.

Ali grabbed Officer Brown. "Please keep him in sight. I think he's been poisoned."

The area filled with officers trying to see what the commotion was. "Grab an evidence bag!" Ali barked to one young man as he walked by. "Don't dump it out. I think there's poison it in and we need the lab to test it."

The officer nodded and carefully bagged the cup. "I'll run it right over to the lab, ma'am." Ali nodded.

The paramedics arrived. Ali pointed to the restroom. "He's in there." She waited anxiously as they brought Wes out on the stretcher. His face had a greenish tinge to it, and other than continued complaints of stomach pains, he seemed to be in no other distress.

She remained behind the paramedics. "I'll follow you."

Wes tried to wave her off, but the gesture was feeble and his eyes pleaded with her to come with him. She nodded and tried to put on a fearless face, yet inside, she was terrified.

They arrived at the hospital in almost no time at all, and the waiting began. It seemed like hours had passed, but in reality, it hadn't been long at all. Ali passed the time waiting for news by calling Sara.

"Sara, it's Ali."

"Hi. Is something wrong? Your voice sounds—"

"Can you come to the hospital and tell no one?"

"Of course," Sara said. "I'll be right there, but will you tell me what's going on?"

Ali sighed. "Wes is here. Apparently, our poisoner tried to take him out. He drank some coffee from a cup because there was a note on it stating it was from you. Signed with just an S like you signed all your notes before."

"Fuck. I'm on my way."

"Sara..."

"Yeah?"

"I'm serious. Tell no one." Ali hung up before Sara could answer.

She must not have been far as Sara arrived within twenty minutes. She ran into the waiting room, disheveled and out of breath. She hadn't been there minutes before the doctor came to find them. Ali was pleased to see it was Dr. Davison—who had already worked on this case with a previous victim. He greeted her and took both her and Sara to a small room off the waiting room to speak privately.

"He's lucky," the doctor said. "He only drank about a quarter of the coffee, which did come back having high levels of arsenic in it. I assume this was an attempt on his life after what we saw with Mr. Mercier."

Ali closed her eyes, offering a brief thank you to the universe. "How long will he be laid up?"

Dr. Davison laughed. "You do know this man, correct? His response to me was *treat me and let me out of here*. We've done an irrigation that should flush the majority of the poison out of his system. He needs to increase his water intake—water, not coffee—and eat high-fiber foods to help eliminate any remaining traces. I'm confident he'll make a full recovery. There wasn't enough to kill him, but had he drunk the full cup of coffee, he wouldn't have been so lucky."

"Can we see him?" Sara asked.

The doctor nodded. "Just down the hall, Room 112. I'll be there in a little bit with discharge papers."

Sara and Ali headed to the room. Wes was sitting up leaning against pillows when they walked in. Ali immediately went over and kissed him. "Thank God you are okay."

Wes held her close. "I didn't see that coming at all."

Sara came close to the bed on the opposite side of Ali. She grabbed Wes's hand and squeezed. "I'm glad you're okay."

He squeezed her hand back and pulled her into a hug. "I'm fine." He reached for Ali with his free hand and held both of them close. As they pulled back, he grimaced. "Not a smart move on my part, I guess, thinking my sister would send me coffee."

Sara grinned. "You should have known I would make you buy your own."

Wes nodded. "But that brings us back to who would know how you sign your notes to me? This is someone I think knows you and obviously is trying to set you up. I think that just solidified that point for me."

Both Ali and Sara looked at him. "You think I know the killer?" Sara asked.

Ali watched as horror passed over Sara's face. She just stared at Wes. Ali turned toward him. "Do you really think that's a possibility?"

Wes scowled. "Unfortunately, since they came after *me*, yeah, I think that is a very strong possibility."

Sara plopped into a chair. "I honestly don't know who would want to do that to me."

Ali sat on the edge of the bed. "Wes, it's not the first time someone has come after you."

His head drew back. "When has someone come after me?"

"It was indirectly, but Katie. She was killed simply because you were helping her back on the hatchet case," Ali reminded him.

"Yes, but that was a direct strike to me."

Ali nodded. "But this is a different killer."

Wes laid his head back on the pillow, fatigue showing in his eyes. "There has to be a reason, though. And every victim has linked to Sara." His weary eyes cut in Sara's direction. "Either through you knowing personally or through your former employer. There has to be a connection to you. Someone is not happy with you, Sis."

"I don't know how I feel about that." Sara groaned. "I have so little friends as it is."

"Who knows how you sign your notes?" Wes demanded.

"No one that I know. I never told anyone I was leaving notes for you."

Ali tilted her head in thought. "Did you write the notes anywhere other than your house? Somewhere that someone could have seen you?"

Sara shook her head. "I usually wrote them in the car outside of Wes's house."

Dr. Davison walked in. "Just me." He smiled at Wes. "Now, how well are you going to follow instructions?"

Wes smirked. "I'm the perfect patient."

The doctor chuckled. "Said only the ones that never followed orders."

Wes sobered. "Seriously, though. I will do what I'm told. Trust me, these two will never forgive me if I don't."

"Amen to that," Ali said as Sara nodded.

"I don't want you leaving for a while. The irrigation can be a bit rough, and I want you to just relax for a couple of hours. Around two p.m. I will sign your discharge papers."

Wes started to protest, but Ali stood up. "That will be just fine."

The doctor pointed at Wes. "You, my friend, will be following orders if this one has anything to say about it."

Wes groaned. "Ain't that the truth."

Once the doctor was gone, Sara offered to go get some food for them. She and Ali discussed what was best for Wes to eat since he was already complaining that hospital food was not going to cut it. They agreed that sandwiches would be fine, and Sara left, promising to be back within an hour.

With Sara gone, Ali slid on top of the bed and sat close with Wes. "You scared me."

"I know. But it's going to take more than that to kill me," he joked.

"Wes, I'm serious. What if I hadn't gotten there

when I did? Would you have drunk the rest of the coffee?" Tears filled Ali's eyes.

"No. I had already taken a couple of antacids, thinking it was the caffeine bothering my stomach. I was switching to water and wouldn't have finished the coffee."

"But that arsenic would have been in your system, and there could have been damage from it."

Wes held her hand. "Yes, but you were there and you jumped right in and saved the day."

"Thanks to Cheryl, really," Ali said.

"What do you mean?"

"I didn't tell you she called a while ago, and she had a vision with you doubled over like in stomach pain. She didn't know if it was a vision of you being sick, or you manifesting what a victim was going through. She had no clear answer to it and didn't want to bother you with it, because you know—you not really believing. So, she called me and I told her I would see when it was the right time to tell you. I honestly forgot about it until I walked in and saw you. It came flooding back, and I knew we had to get you to the hospital." The words rushed out of Ali.

"Well, I'm glad you knew. Maybe there is something to Cheryl's visions. I'm not convinced, but I'm definitely not saying she's a loony." He smiled at Ali. "I love you."

forty-two

Ali got Dawson home and settled. It had been a long day before the doctor finally released them late afternoon. Ali had called out of work for the day so she could be with him and bring him home, although Dawson had begged her not to. He had other thoughts about settling down and just relaxing. He had wanted her to run by the station so he could pick up the folder and things he had been working on. She refused.

She did, however, concede to text Brown and ask him to bring the files to Dawson. She seemed to think if Brown was there, maybe Dawson would stay put. He felt fine, but Ali hovered around him.

Usually, she wasn't that type of person, but Dawson couldn't blame her. If the roles had been reversed, he would be doing the same thing. He was mad at himself for allowing a deranged killer to get so close to him. He should have known better than to drink the coffee. Sara wouldn't have been at the station early enough to give him coffee. Would she have even known what time he would have arrived that morning? His sleep-deprived mind apparently had not picked up on any of that, and he just saw coffee and needed the caffeine.

Dawson hadn't been home long when someone knocked on the door. He heard Brown's low voice talking with Ali in the hallway before Brown appeared in the living room.

"Some people will do anything to get out of work," Brown quipped as he placed a folder next to Dawson.

"Get out of work?" Dawson grinned and pointed at the folder. "You're still dropping things off for me."

"Yeah, I can't win. You realize you have put me in a very difficult position. Ali is ready to kill me for bringing you work, and *you* would kill me if I didn't bring it." Brown rolled his eyes.

"Sit down and let's talk about this," Dawson said, and once Brown was settled, Dawson continued. "How did the killer walk into the station and no one see her?"

Brown shook his head. "I don't know. I talked to the guys on duty. She must have planned it perfectly. They were either in the restroom, off getting coffee, or at someone's desk, talking. It had been a quiet night, so they weren't hanging out at their desks."

"Too damn close, Brown." Dawson stared out the living room door into the kitchen. He couldn't see Ali but could hear her moving about in the kitchen. When upset, she tended to cook. So, the good thing that came out of all the mess, Dawson knew there would be something yummy to munch on later. Something much better than the sandwiches Sara had brought him at the hospital.

"How's Sara taking this?" Brown asked.

Dawson raised an eyebrow. "She's okay. Handling it like a trooper. But you probably should check on her later."

Brown narrowed his eyes at Dawson. "Is that permission or sarcasm?"

Dawson shrugged. "Maybe a bit of both."

Dawson flipped open the file and stared at the contents. "No connection between the fifth victim and the others, other than delivering clean linens to the convention center after the fact. There has to be something we're missing."

Frustration filled the air as Dawson threw the file down on the floor and stood up. "Come on."

Brown followed him into the kitchen.

"Wait a minute." Ali's voice stopped them. "Where do you think you're going?" "Just moving around," Dawson said. "Don't worry I'm not leaving the house." He gave her a kiss. "But I can't sit still and think. I need to move."

"Fine. Go out back and walk around the yard." Ali turned to Brown. "Seriously, Kyle, do not let him do anything he shouldn't be doing."

Brown nodded as Dawson turned toward him. "Kyle?"

"Yes, sir."

"Your name's *Kyle*? How did I not know that?"

Brown laughed. "Because you never introduced me to your sister."

Dawson scoffed and headed for the back door. "Come on." Brown sat down on a chair as Dawson paced around the yard.

"What do we know?"

"No real links other than those between the three wives on the board," Brown answered. "Sara isn't linked to only the first one, really."

"Wait..." Dawson stopped pacing. "What if this was all to put us off the track? My coffee this morning was made to look like it was from Sara."

"Yes?"

"What if the killer knows Sara?"

"I thought we went down that road."

"We did, but we didn't really go far with it." Dawson started toward the house. "What if *Sara* is in danger?"

forty-three

I straightened my wig. I specifically chose the outfit I was wearing as one I knew Sara would recognize. Designer jeans and a jade-colored sweater that clung to me in the right places. I made sure I had my last vial. This one was specifically for Sara. It had a little more than the others. I wanted to watch it hit her hard and fast.

I arrived at her place and knocked on the door. When she opened it, she looked like she had been crying. "What—"

I pushed into the apartment and cut her off before she could say another word.

"Time to sit down, Sara, and have a chat." I pulled

a gun from my purse and trained it on her. She just nodded and sat down on the couch.

"What are you doing?" she asked.

"I'm taking over...your business, your life. And you, my dear, are going to do a couple of things for me." A thrill shot through me as fear filled her eyes.

I grabbed her phone from the table, just as it sounded. It opened as I lifted it to my face and smiled. *Well, the facial ID worked.* "Oh, a text from your brother." *I thought he would be dead and out of my way by now.* I kept my face neutral. "*Are you okay?*" *Oh, he sounds concerned.*

"Let me answer him or he will end up coming here."

"Oh, I don't think so. I think I'm perfectly capable of answering a text from your brother. Besides, I doubt he's in any shape to come to your rescue right now."

Sara tilted her head at me. "No? Guess you hadn't heard. Your attempt on his life didn't work. He's home from the hospital and doing just fine."

Fuck. I quickly typed off a reply to Dawson. *I'm good.*

"Why are you doing this?" Sara asked.

I laughed. "Why? You have had everything handed to you, and honestly, I'm just sick of it. You have taken and lived a good life." I swept my arms around her place.

She started to interrupt, but I waved the gun at her. "Just shut up. I don't want to hear from you. You are going to just sit there and listen."

I started pacing around the living room. My heels tapping a beat as I moved about on the hardwood floor. "You don't even know how much you took from me. All these years, things just kept falling in your lap. I have been sitting back and watching, and losing out."

My voice seemed to echo in the quietness. Sara was

sitting very still, watching me. "What do you mean I took things from you?"

My stomach rolled at the oblivion she portrayed. "You didn't know that I applied to work for Madame, did you?"

She shook her head.

"I was told I wasn't pretty enough...and yet, here I am looking just like you. We could be twins." I tilted my head. "Did you know Sam broke up with me because he just wanted you?"

A horrified look came across her face. "Oh, yes, and then there was Daniel who also broke up with me because he set up a date with you. Thought he could weasel into your business and have you as a side piece."

"But I didn't know the others you killed—and I didn't know Daniel. He told me his name was Sawyer."

"Doesn't matter. They all pushed me aside for you. And Michael, you may not remember him, but he knew you. Even when I dressed like this, looking just like you, he pushed me away and rejected me. I know you took Madame's books and you did nothing with them. You could have grown that business into so much more, instead you focused on one or two men and that was it. *Pathetic*."

"You're sick," Sara said, disgust rolling off her tongue.

I waved the gun at her. "Maybe, but I'm going to have a great life once you are out of the picture. I'm taking over this apartment, your life, your business."

"You will never be me. You have a black heart."

I laughed. "I'll take that as a compliment, my dear." I waved the gun at her. "Come on. Over to the table."

Sara moved to the table, and I sat her down, tying her legs to the chair's and her left arm to the back of the chair. I left her right arm free so she could write her suicide note. I then went to the kitchen and made her a cup of coffee.

I set the coffee and a piece of paper in front of her. "You will write a suicide note to your brother. Tell him you couldn't deal with the fact that he was disappointed with you."

"He's not disappointed with me," Sara broke in.

"Well, that is what you believe he is. So just write it." I sneered at her.

She picked up the pen. I positioned the paper for her, and then taped it to the table so it wouldn't move as she wrote. She began:

Wes,

I am so sorry it came to this. I wish I had had the courage to reach out to you sooner and forget all this nonsense of thinking you would be disappointed. You have always been a terrible little brother, but I have loved you with all my heart.

˜S

Sara sat back and stared at the letter.

"Really? That's all you have to say to a brother you haven't spoken to in years and now is your chance to say so much?"

"Well, like you said, I haven't spoken to him in years. I wrote what I needed to say to him. It's not like we're that close anymore." Sara shrugged.

I wasn't sure I believed her, but I didn't really care, either. I put the vial next to the coffee cup. She eyed it warily.

"You will get to experience what all those men went through because they pissed me off," I said with a satisfied grin.

"What about the others that died? Who were they to you?"

"They were all men that had rejected me. Even the last one, Erik. He was my boyfriend from years ago.

He could have taken me off the streets when he won a little bit of money. Instead, he left me like a gutter rat and went on with a new life. Got a job, an apartment...a new girlfriend. It was time to take out the trash on all those men."

"You *are* sick," Sara said, repeating what she'd said earlier with even more disgust.

I opened the vial and carefully poured it into the coffee. I watched it dissolve in the hot liquid and pushed the cup toward her. "It's time. You need to drink up."

"Or what? Are you going to pour it down my throat if I refuse? Just shoot me and get it over it."

"And make a mess in my new apartment?" I laughed.

forty-four

Dawson and Brown both ran for the door when Dawson mentioned Sara might be in danger. "Got to get to Sara's. Call her, please!" Dawson yelled to Ali as they ran to the cars.

"I'll call for backup!" Brown yelled as he raced to his car.

They sped through the streets. Dawson's heart squeezed as he feared the worst for his sister...his sister, he had just found her and couldn't lose her again. *This damn killer.* He hadn't even seen it and the signs were all in front of him. He had come face to face with her.

They arrived at Sara's apartment in record time.

Brown and Dawson took the stairs two at a time and paused outside the door. Dawson could hear Sara's phone ringing. He pressed his ear to the door, hoping he could hear whether or not Sara answered.

"Hi, Ali... No everything is fine... Oh, just call him and tell him he doesn't need to stop by. I'm tired from today and just want to take a nap."

Sara sounded fine, but something was off. Dawson just knew it. He pointed to Brown and mouthed, "*You knock. Don't let her know I'm here.*" Dawson took a few steps back away from the door and into the shadows.

Brown held his gun behind his back and knocked. Suddenly, the door opened.

"Hi, Kyle," a female voice said. "What are you doing here?"

"I just wanted to check on you," Brown answered, but Dawson could tell that the woman wasn't Sara, and he assumed he knew exactly who she was. "With everything that happened to Wes, I figured you might want some company." Surely, Brown knew she wasn't really Sara.

"That's sweet, but I'm good. I'm just wiped out and want to take a nap. Can we talk later?" She started to shut the door, but Brown put his foot against it and stepped into the room.

Dawson rushed in right behind him, gun raised. They took the girl off guard for a moment, but she recovered quickly and moved behind Sara at the kitchen table in an instant. She pointed a gun at Sara's head.

"Hi, Kyle, Wes. Glad you could join the party," Sara quipped. She sounded lighthearted, but Dawson could see the fear in her eyes. He noticed a cup of coffee on the table and an empty vial next to it.

"Surprised to see me, Evie?" Dawson asked.

Evie looked at him wide-eyed. "I thought being the coffee-aholic you are that you would be long gone, so yes I am a bit surprised."

"I want to know how you got in the station without anyone noticing you." Dawson trained his gun on Evie's head.

"Oh, that was easy. In fact, I *was* noticed, but I had made sure to dress like Sara and one of the young men even said, *hi, Sara,* to me as I walked by going to your desk. You cops really can't see what's right in front of you." Evie laughed.

Dawson glanced down at the table and saw a note in front of Sara. "Suicide note?"

Evie nodded. "I thought it was a nice touch, but apparently, your sister doesn't have much to say to you." She frowned. "This is a predicament, isn't it? I only have one vial left and that one is tagged for Sara. I guess I'm going to have to waste two bullets on you two fine officers."

"You think you can shoot both of us before we take you down?" Brown asked. He kept glancing at Sara.

"Oh, I can get one of you for sure. The other may get me, but the ultimate goal here is to get rid of this bitch."

She pushed the gun against Sara's head. "Drink up, dear."

Sara looked at Dawson, her eyes pleading with him to help her.

Evie scowled. "I will pour it down your throat, if I have to."

Sara glanced up at her. "No. I'm not drinking it."

Evie hit her with the gun, not hard enough to knock her out, but enough to stun Sara. "Drink."

Dawson stared at Sara and shook his head *no*.

Sara's hand trembled as she picked up the cup. She looked at Dawson, and then directly at Brown.

"Don't drink it, Sara," Brown pleaded.

Dawson and Brown each took another step closer to Evie. "Don't move another inch or I will just shoot her," Evie warned.

Sara flung the coffee up toward Evie's face and ducked. The coffee hit Evie's eyes. She instinctively lowered the gun to try and wipe off her face. Dawson grabbed the gun from her. Brown immediately hand-cuffed Evie's hands behind her back while Dawson untied Sara.

Sara flung her arms around Dawson and hung on. "Thank God you showed up."

Sara released Dawson and turned toward Evie. "Why? Why did you have to do all this?"

Evie shrugged. "I was just searching for the perfect mate—the real romance of life. And it just always gravitated toward you." A tear ran down her cheek.

Dawson took hold of her arm and moved her toward the door as he started reciting the Miranda rights. He glanced back and smiled.

Brown was holding Sara in his arms, and she clutched at him even more firmly than she had held onto Dawson.

He let out a relieved breath—knowing Sara was going to be all right in more than one way—and put his attention on the criminal beside him. He didn't un-derstand how anyone could harbor so much hate.

He did his job and led Evie out the door.

Things could have ended much worse.

about the author

E.L. REED moved to Tennessee after living in New Hampshire all her life. She has fond memories of the Maine coastline and incorporates the ocean into all her books. She has three grown children and is enjoying her empty nest. Her life has been touched and changed by her son's autism - she views life through a very different lens than before he was born. Growing up as an avid reader, it was only natural for Emma Leigh to turn to creating the stories for others to enjoy. Emma Leigh continues to learn through her children's strength and abilities that pushes her to go outside her comfort zone on a regular basis. She has also authored romantic suspense, women's fiction and co-authored children's books. She shares her love for writing as an English Professor at a local community college.

elreedauthor.com

ALSO AVAILABLE IN THE
MEMORIES OF MURDER
NOVEL SERIES

Available whereever you
purchase your bookds.

Also avaiable in audiobook.

one

The moon created long shadows between the buildings and gave the perfect cover. I darted in and out, becoming one with the shadows. My movements were hurried as anxiety rose within me, only to be outweighed by the confidence bubbling up.

I stopped and glanced into the alley before entering at a slower pace, darting my eyes from side to side, taking everything in.

The reek of urine and body odor took my breath away, and I paused. The stench of the alley didn't deter me. Instead, it spurred me on. Pressed against the wall, I blended further into the darkness and spotted him. The perfect target. The homeless man walking to the dumpster, his movements slow as he lumbered toward it and laid down his backpack next to it. This man would be the quintessential guinea pig for my plan.

He squatted by his bag to pull out a jacket, then carefully zipped up the backpack. He flailed the coat out in front of him, opening it up. My adrenaline kicked in, and I could hardly restrain myself as I watched him slide his arm into the sleeve.

I crept closer, hugging the wall. My fingers twitched around the handle with anticipation. My heart raced and I heard the rush of blood pounding in my head like a drum. The man's movements were slow, no indication that he was worried about anything around him.

I held my breath as I took another step closer, then exhaled slowly, trying to calm my racing heart. The shadows were perfectly placed, hiding my movements. I crept out from the wall, just a step away from him.

I raised my arm and brought my hatchet down with as much force as I could. The first blow struck the back of the man's neck. It hit with a greater force than I had anticipated, the blade cutting deep. His blood spattered my face and hand. The warmth of it shocked me but triggered an adrenaline rush I didn't expect as he fell to his knees.

I brought my arm back for another swing, the enticing sensation of his blood fueling me on. The second blow took him forward, face down on the ground. Since my goal was his face, I turned him over with my foot. I had a haunting urge, to mutilate the faces that haunted my dreams. And, although he was simply a guinea pig, I needed to see how erasing a face could empty my dreams...*my nightmares.*

With my right foot on his stomach, I rained blow after blow upon his face until he was no longer recognizable.

After ten strikes—or was it eleven—I stood back and surveyed my surroundings. Blood pooled beneath the man's head. Satisfied with my accomplishment, I glanced down at myself. His splattered blood covered me from head to toe. A peace settled over me at how easy it had been to take the man's life. Easy because I didn't know him? Or easy because I was finally strong enough to fight back?

I used the man's cloths to wipe off the excessive blood from the hatchet blade and carefully stepped away to avoid the pool of blood on the ground. With one more glance, I turned and hurried from the alley, staying in the shadows and out of sight.

Entering a small door in the wall, I stood still for a moment. I allowed my eyes to adjust to the darkness, then continued down a corridor until I reached the lone room at the end of the hall. There was no electricity. Only a faint beam of moonlight streamed into the center of the room from a small window near the ceiling.

A cot at the far wall stood with only a threadbare blanket across it. No pillow. The opposite wall held a little table with a single chair. I crossed the room to the table and picked up a rag, then ran it over the hatchet, clearing it of the man's hair, skin, and blood. My fingers lovingly stroked the fine weapon. This was the power I'd been searching for. For years, I didn't know how it would make me feel. But tonight, I felt a strength within I never imagined would emerge. Satisfied, I laid the hatchet on the table.

Under a candleholder at its center was a piece of paper with a black crayon next to it. I slid the paper out, picked up the crayon, and drew a thick black line through the first item on the list. After carefully placing the paper back under the candlestick, I peeled off my dark cloak and changed into clean clothes from the closet, then stuffed the blood-soaked cloak and clothing into a garbage bag. Once I cleaned my face and neck from the blood spatter, I threw the wet cloth I used into the bag with the other blood-stained items.

Inhaling deeply and exhaling slowly, I calmed my racing heart.

One down.

A smile curled up the corners of my mouth, and I gave myself a virtual pat on the back for pulling off the first—and most difficult—kill I'd have on this journey. I cautiously opened the door and ran along the hall toward the exit leading to the street.

With a quick glance around me, I exited the place and ran, careful to stay close to the wall of the buildings, blending in with the shadows, indiscernible to the world. I loved being able to disappear into an alley and from sight.

Releasing a sigh of relief, I mingled with the homeless wandering around, then crept away unnoticed. I vanished into my little world where no one knew if I was alive or not, except to kick me when I was down. There'd be a change with that. No more would I tolerate those kicks. I wasn't taking the abuse anymore. I had found my voice, and those who'd hurt me in any way had better watch out.

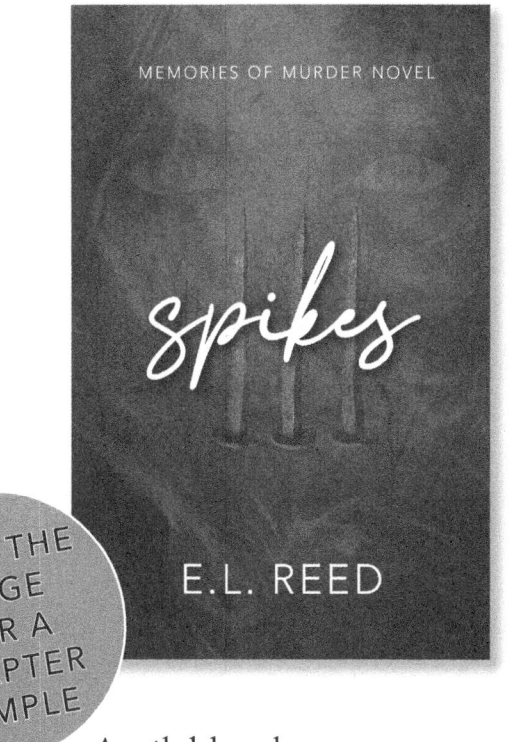

prologue

Two years prior...

I had just been hired at this quaint bed-and-breakfast. The inn was just getting ready to open for the upcoming season, and today I had the opportunity to get familiar with my new place. I was giddy with excitement to start this new journey.

I explored the second floor, peeking in at all the rooms. Then I went to the first floor and checked out the back rooms off the kitchen. There were three bedrooms and a storage room; me, the housekeeper, and the cook would sleep here. Off the main foyer—where the registration desk stood—was a living room where a fireplace was in the center of two, floor-to-ceiling bookcases. The living room on the backside of the house had ceiling-to-floor windows that opened onto a deck overlooking the ocean. The deck was going to be my favorite place. I just knew it.

I moved to the other side of the foyer. One room on this main floor was positioned almost under the stairs, but extended away from the house. The owner had instructed that this particular room was not to be used unless the inn was full.

I wandered in and glanced around. The room was small, but it had a spectacular view from the windows. I would consider this the best room in the house. I curiously moved around it. The closet was long, as opposed to *wide*, which seemed odd, but it went under the stair access, so I assumed that was the reason. I adjusted some hangers on the rack.

As I turned to step back out of the closet, my toe caught on a bump in the floor. I bent to inspect it and found a small section of the flooring that did not fit into the tongue and groove. I tried to push it in, and when I couldn't budge it, I pulled it up. The floor lifted as one piece in a large square in my hand and revealed a trap door. I pushed the section of floor back out of the way and opened the trap door. I held my breath, expecting a large creak as the door pulled up.

Silence.

I grabbed my cell phone to turn on the flashlight and peered down. Stone stairs descended circularly. I couldn't see beyond that. I heard Minnie, the housekeeper, who crept around silently—hence the mousy nickname—moving around in the living room. It spurred me to put the trap door back down and pull the flooring into place. I made a mental note to get a small runner over this flooring section to keep a guest from tripping over it.

I decided to make a return trip tonight to explore

what was below the room. A chill of excitement ran through me, and an unexplained feeling of déjà vu came over me. I shook my head and headed for the living room.

The day dragged on as I helped Minnie with the bedrooms, prepping for the five rooms that would be used tomorrow night. I then checked on Ramsay in the kitchen to see if he was prepared for the cocktail hour, offered with small hors d'oeuvres and breakfast. It was the understanding of the guests arriving that if they wished to order dinner some night, they needed to give twenty-four-hours' notice for the meal, other-wise, after cocktails and hors d'oeuvres, they would go into town to eat at a local restaurant.

After Minnie and Ramsay, the cook, had gone to bed, and I knew they would be asleep, I crept out of my room and made my way to Room 1. I carried a pair of sneakers in my hand to put on in the room. I didn't know what to expect at the bottom of those stairs.

With shoes on and the trap door open, I pulled out my cell phone and flipped on the flashlight. I cautiously started down the stone stairs. The walls, also made of stone, were rough as I ran my hand along the wall while descending the circular stairway. It had no railing, and the stone was cold under my fingers. The air got colder and damper the farther down I went. When I arrived at the bottom of the stairs, I saw a short hallway leading to a door to my left. Straight across from the stairs was a room. As I stepped into it, an icy feeling ran over me, and I shivered from the intensity of it.

This room had tracks on the floor, a hose to one

side, and a table on the back wall. Next to the table was another door. I went to it first and opened it. It was a closet lined with empty, dusty shelves. They obviously hadn't been used for a long time. I turned toward the bench and saw a box with a red button on it. I picked it up and pushed the button. A small whirling sound startled me, and I spun around to find spikes rising out of the floor.

A stabbing pain shot through my head above my eyes, and I dropped the controller. It landed with a clatter, snapping me out of the pain. I bent to pick it up. As I rose and set it on the table, I studied the bed of spikes. There were five strategically placed, with three in a row and two more that were spread out lower than the lined ones and laid out perpendicularly to the others. I walked around them and noticed on the floor, not only the tracks where the bed of spikes could come out or nest back in there, but also a drainage hole where water could drain.

I shook my head. A feeling of giddiness overtook me as a flash of a young man lying on those spikes, *dead*, invaded my mind. I stared at the sharp, lethal points and carefully ran my hand down one of the iron rods. I glanced up at the ceiling above the spikes and saw where there was a section cut out with hinges to the side like that of a door.

I had such a feeling of familiarity in this place, yet I shook it off. Before I left the room, I pushed the button to lower the spikes back into the floor. I went to the door at the end of the hallway and opened it, discovering a small path between the cliff and the house. I closed the door again.

Hmm. . .

I contemplated all I'd seen and retraced my steps back upstairs. This job just got a whole lot more interesting.

ALSO AVAILABLE FROM
EMMA LEIGH REED

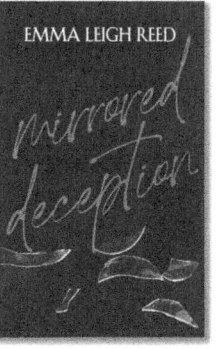

AVAILABLE WHEREVER
YOU BUY BOOKS

Made in the USA
Columbia, SC
08 November 2023